What Kids Say About Carole Marsh Mysteries . . .

I love the real locations! Reading the book always makes me want to go and visit them all on our next family vacation. My Mom says maybe, but I can't wait!

One day, I want to be a real kid in one of Ms. Marsh's mystery books. I think it would be fun, and I think I am a real character anyway. I filled out the application and sent it in and am keeping my fingers crossed!

History was not my favorite subject till I starting reading Carole Marsh Mysteries. Ms. Marsh really brings history to life. Also, she leaves room for the scary and fun.

I think Christina is so smart and brave. She is lucky to be in the mystery books because she gets to go to a lot of places. I always wonder just how much of the book is true and what is made up. Trying to figure that out is fun!

Grant is cool and funny! He makes me laugh a lot!!

I like that there are boys and girls in the story of different ages. Some mysteries I outgrow, but I can always find a favorite character to identify with in these books.

They are scary, but not too scary. They are funny. I learn a lot. There is always food which makes me hungry. I feel like I am there.

What Adults Say About Carole Marsh Mysteries . . .

I think kids love these books because they have such a wealth of detail. I know I learn a lot reading them! It's an engaging way to look at the history of any place or event. I always say I'm only going to read one chapter to the kids, but that never happens—it's always two or three, at least!   —Librarian

Reading the mystery and going on the field trip—Scavenger Hunt in hand—was the most fun our class ever had! It really brought the place and its history to life. They loved the real kids characters and all the humor. I loved seeing them learn that reading is an experience to enjoy!   —4th grade teacher

Carole Marsh is really on to something with these unique mysteries. They are so clever; kids want to read them all. The Teacher's Guides are chock full of activities, recipes, and additional fascinating information. My kids thought I was an expert on the subject—and with this tool, I felt like it!   —3rd grade teacher

My students loved writing their own Real Kids/Real Places mystery book! Ms. Marsh's reproducible guidelines are a real jewel. They learned about copyright and more & ended up with their own book they were so proud of!   —Reading/Writing Teacher

The Mystery in
NEW YORK CITY

by
Carole Marsh

Editorial Assistant: Steven St. Laurent

Cover design: Vicki DeJoy; Editor: Chad Beard; Graphic Design: Steve
St. Laurent; Layout and footer design: Lynette Rowe; Photography: Michael
Boylan.

Gallopade International is introducing SAT words that kids need to know in each new book
that we publish. The SAT words are bold in the story. Look for this special logo
beside each word in the glossary. Happy Learning!

Gallopade is proud to be a member and supporter of these educational organizations and associations:

American Booksellers Association
American Library Association
International Reading Association
National Association for Gifted Children
The National School Supply and Equipment Association
The National Council for the Social Studies
Museum Store Association
Association of Partners for Public Lands
Association of Booksellers for Children
Association for the Study of African American Life and History
National Alliance of Black School Educators

This book is dedicated to Ellen and Luke, the two cutest kids in the world! One day we'll take you to the city so nice they named it twice!

– *SS*

For additional information on Carole Marsh Mysteries, visit: www.carolemarshmysteries.com

We love the Big Apple!

30 YEARS AGO . . .

As a mother and an author, one of the fondest periods of my life was when I decided to write mystery books for children. At this time (1979) kids were pretty much glued to the TV, something parents and teachers complained about the way they do about video games today.

I decided to set each mystery in a real place—a place kids could go and visit for themselves after reading the book. And I also used real children as characters. Usually a couple of my own children served as characters, and I had no trouble recruiting kids from the book's location to also be characters.

Also, I wanted all the kids—boys and girls of all ages—to participate in solving the mystery. And, I wanted kids to learn something as they read. Something about the history of the location. And I wanted the stories to be funny.

That formula of real+scary+smart+fun served me well. The kids and I had a great time visiting each site and many of the events in the stories actually came out of our experiences there. (For example, Grant and Christina's grandmother really did come through Ellis Island as an immigrant when she was just a little girl!)

I love getting letters from teachers and parents who say they read the book with their class or child, then visited the historic site and saw all the places in the mystery for themselves. What's so great about that? What's great is that you and your children have an experience that bonds you together forever. Something you shared. Something you both cared about at the time. Something that crossed all age levels—a good story, a good scare, a good laugh!

30 years later,

Carole Marsh

Christina Yother   **Grant Yother**   **Cyrus Akbari**   **Heather Ellis**

ABOUT THE CHARACTERS

Christina Yother, 9, from Peachtree City, Georgia

Grant Yother, 7, from Peachtree City, Georgia
Christina's brother

Cyrus Akbari as Binyamin (Benjamin), 11, from New
    York City

Heather Ellis as Katarzyna (Katherine), 10, from
    Poland

Many of the places featured in the book actually exist and
are worth a visit! Perhaps you could read the book and see some
of the places the kids visited during their mysterious adventure!

Titles in the Carole Marsh Mysteries Series

Books and Teacher's Guides are available at booksellers, libraries, school supply stores, museums, and many other locations!

CONTENTS

1 PACK YOUR BAGS!

"Start spreadin' the news. . . " Christina heard someone singing. She paused in the hallway at the door to Grant's bedroom. Grant was singing as he dug around in his dresser for clothes to pack. A pair of khaki shorts flew over his shoulder and landed on the bed.

"I'm leavin' today. . . " Another pair of shorts, blue jeans this time, sailed across the room.

"I wanna be a part of it. . . " One last pair of shorts atop the pile and Grant closed the drawer.

"New York! New York!" he shouted as he turned toward the closet to select his shirts. Christina smiled as she walked into the room.

"Are you having fun packing?" she asked.

Grant turned from the closet with a small armload of shirts. He nodded as he continued humming the song.

I'm Leavin' Today. . .

New York, New York!

1

"Are you almost done?" Christina asked. "It's time for dinner, you know."

"I just have to pack my underpants," Grant chirped. He tossed the shirts into a suitcase, hangers and all. Christina scrunched up her nose at the thought of underpants, anyone's, clean or not. And you never knew with Grant's, since he was always jumbling up his clean and dirty laundry!

"Well, Mimi and Papa are here," Christina said, "and we're putting dinner on the table, so c'mon."

As they made their way to the dining room, Grant belted out, "NEW YORK, NE-EW YOOORK!!"

Papa greeted them at the dining room archway. "Hey, Christina! Hey, Grant! How are you? Ready to go to the Big Apple?"

"To the city that doesn't sleep?" Mimi appeared from the kitchen. "Hey, kids! Are you ready?"

"YES!" they shouted in stereo.

"I have everything we need right here," Christina smiled. She proudly presented a red three-ring binder. It was stuffed with all sorts of things for their trip.

"It's got the field journal my teacher gave me, brochures from historic sites in the city, and even subway route maps."

New York.
New York!

Time for
Dinner!

"All neatly organized, I'll bet," Papa said, knowing Christina's everything-in-its-place way of doing things.

"Yes, sir!" she assured him.

"Are we going to eat?" Grant asked. "Singing makes me hungry!"

Everyone ate quickly, as if there was a big rush, but they were all packed and ready to fly to New York City the next morning. Everyone was excited about the trip. And, to make it more special—they would be there on the 4th of July! A local friend had arranged for them to watch the fireworks extravaganza from a chartered riverboat.

"The 4th of July fireworks display is going to be spectacular!" Mimi said.

"Breathtaking!" Christina said.

"Cool!" Grant piped in.

"LOUD!" grumbled Papa.

"Did you know," Papa asked, "that the fireworks display in New York City has been presented since 1800?"

"The first Independence Day fireworks display was in Philadelphia," Christina reported, "in 1777."

"That's very good, Christina," Mimi said. "So, do you know where we're going? All the places, I mean?"

Time for Dinner!

New York Fireworks

"Yes, it's all in my notebook."

"I thought it was a binder," Grant said.

"I can call it a notebook since it has a notebook in it," Christina said. Sometimes her little brother could be so. . . little brothery! "Anyway, I planned out subway routes and bus routes to and from all of the places we'll be going to."

"We won't be taking subways or buses," Papa said. "We have transportation for the whole time we're there. Ben's uncle is a taxi driver, and he has a special van for tourists. We'll get to see New York City the nitty-gritty way it needs to be seen—up close and personal—from the streets!"

Christina felt a little frustrated by that. She had worked so hard planning their trips around the city. But Mimi *had* said that the subway—one of the oldest in the world, and the largest in North America—was its own underground world. She also said that they really didn't need to spend much time down there. Mimi did *not* like to be 'underground'.

"We'll get to see *everything*!" Grant giggled. "Not just those smelly old subway trains!"

Christina sighed. All that hard work, she thought. But she knew that Papa and Mimi and Grant were right.

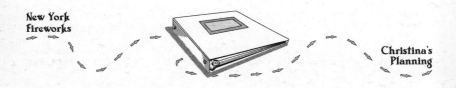

New York
Fireworks

Christina's
Planning

They were going to the greatest city in the world, and they shouldn't have to look at subways all the time.

Besides, they were going to New York for Christina's summer project and Mimi's mystery book research. Mimi probably wouldn't want to write a mystery about the subway or anything that happened on it!

Later, as they left to spend the night at Mimi and Papa's house, they gave hugs and kisses to Mom and Dad, and listened to all the parental advice: "Listen to Mimi and Papa; remember to wash your hands whenever you can; don't take off by yourselves; and stay out of trouble!"

Christina was slightly amused by the one phrase that always followed all the others: "Don't go getting involved in any crazy mysteries!"

As they fell asleep that night, dreaming of skyscrapers, taxicabs, and alligators in the sewers, they had no idea what was in store for them this time!

Christina's Planning

Parental Advice

2 LEAVIN' ON A JET PLANE

Christina looked past Grant out the window of the jet airliner that was in line for takeoff. All she could see was tarmac and grass and little yellow signs. Across the aisle, Papa marveled at the hustle and bustle at the terminals of the busy Atlanta airport. Planes, trucks, baggage carts, and people everywhere!

"I hope we get to see Stone Mountain as we take off," Grant said. "Do you remember when we saw the Christmas tree on top of the mountain?"

"I do! That was so neat!" Christina said.

They heard the jet's engines get louder, and the plane rolled forward and turned. Now they were looking down the runway, where a huge plane was hurtling away from them and lifting its nose into the sky.

"Wow!" Grant exclaimed. "That's even better than

Atlanta
Airport

Taking Off!

7

seeing them from the highway!"

Christina smiled. Planes landing at Hartsfield International Airport flew *very* low over Interstate 85. They both had shrieked in terror the first time a 727 crossed the highway right in front of their speeding car!

The plane's engines got louder, then the aircraft turned again, and aimed down the runway. Christina held onto the armrests with a strong grip. Grant's eyes opened as wide as they could. The engines got really loud, and the big plane lurched forward, forcing everyone back into their seats.

"Hee hee hee!" Grant laughed, as their plane sped faster and faster down the runway and lifted off into the sky.

Almost the second after they were off the ground, Christina was thumbing through a New York City tourist's guidebook. "Hey, Grant," she said, "do you know how many taxicabs there are in New York City?"

"A million?" Grant responded.

"'There are more than 12,000 Yellow Cabs in New York'," Christina quoted from her guidebook, or "survival guide," as Mimi called it.

"Where do they park at night?" Grant wondered aloud.

Taking Off!

Guidebook
Info

"Do you know how old the subway system is?" Christina asked.

"Ummmm. . . one hundred years old?"

"That's right, Grant!" Christina beamed proudly. Grant smiled.   Christina knew her brother was smart, especially when it came to remembering tidbits of trivia.

"Do you know how tall the Empire State building is?" Grant asked Christina, hoping she hadn't marked that page in her survival guide. She hadn't—but she had already written it in her field journal.

"One thousand four hundred fifty-four feet," she proclaimed, "with the mast."

"Mast? Like on a sailboat?" Grant looked confused.

"No, silly," Christina said. "It's a big, giant radio and TV tower."

"Christina," Papa called from across the aisle. "The mast was originally designed to be a mooring for zeppelins."

"For *what*?" Christina and Grant asked.

"Zeppelins!" Papa said.   "Big blimps that used to carry passengers."

Christina was amazed. She could picture a huge blimp hovering above the Empire State Building, but she just couldn't see how people would get off.

Guidebook
Info

Blimps?

"How did the passengers get down?" she asked.

Papa laughed. "There never were any passengers. They discovered that it was too tricky to tie an airship to the top of the building. It was too windy."

Christina wrote everything Papa said in her field journal. "I didn't know that! Thanks, Papa!"

Papa smiled and went back to reading his magazine. Grant watched the patchwork quilt of land below glide by. Mimi slept. Christina read her guidebook, searching for the next interesting trivia fact she could ask Grant.

"I see city down there!" Grant exclaimed. They had been flying for about two hours. Christina looked out the window at the amazing sight—Manhattan Island filled with skyscrapers that looked so tiny from way up high.

Just then, the pilot spoke over the intercom. "Ladies and gentlemen, we'll be landing at LaGuardia International in just a little while. If you look out the port side—the left side—of the aircraft, you'll be able to see Manhattan and the Statue of Liberty. Currently, the weather in New York City is sunny and warm. Enjoy the rest of your flight, folks."

Grant immediately glued his nose to the window.

Blimps?

Over The City

Christina busied herself packing her books. After the plane turned and began its ear-popping descent, Christina crammed herself up next to Grant so she could see out the window, too. But Grant squirmed around so only he could see out the whole window.

"There it is!" Grant shouted. "The Statue of Liberty!"

Christina finally moved him aside and got her first glimpse at Lady Liberty. The gray-green statue was beautifully framed by the lush green of Liberty Island and the deep blue waters of New York Harbor.

"Wow!" Christina exclaimed. "It's beautiful! And, it's the first place we're going!"

Over The City

Statue Of Liberty

3 MYSTERY VAN WITH A VIEW

LaGuardia Airport was awash in noise from thousands of people talking and laughing, kids yelling and babies crying, baggage being thrown around, announcements blaring over the public address system—Christina thought it would probably be quieter out on the tarmac with the planes!

"Christina! Grant! Over here!" came a shout through the **cacophony**. They turned to see who was calling them. A boy with spiky hair and big brown eyes jogged toward them.

"Hi, Ben!" Christina called back and waved. Ben skidded to a halt in front of them. He gave Christina a big hug and a kiss on both cheeks.

"Hi Grant!" Ben reached out his hand and shook Grant's with a crushing grip.

LaGuardia
Airport

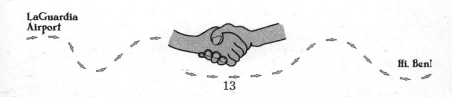

Hi, Ben!

13

"Ow! Hi. . ." Grant muttered.

"Binyamin!" Mimi greeted him. "Shalom!"

"Shalom!" he replied, then greeted Papa and shook his hand.

Christina was always excited to see Ben, or Binyamin, his Jewish name. His family honored all the Jewish customs, even though his mother was a full-blooded Italian. That always made for an interesting Hanukkah/Christmas season!

Ben was two years older than Christina. He had stayed with Christina and Grant on a month-long student exchange program a couple of years earlier. He had also changed a lot since the last time they had seen each other. That probably was why Grant was staring at him like he'd never seen him before.

"Hey, you guys!" a heavily accented voice from the past shouted. "It's good to see you again! I thought you'd never get here! It's been so long! How long has it been? Years! I can't believe it!"

Ben's Mom, Viviana, with arms outstretched, came bursting through a steady river of people to the little island the group had formed. A young girl about Christina's age, whom they had never met, trailed behind her.

Christina braced for another round of hugging and

Hi, Ben!   Ben's Mom

kissing and shaking hands. Grant tried to hide behind his bag, but he still got a big smacker of a kiss from Ben's Mom.

"Guys, this is Katarzyna," Viviana introduced the girl, pronouncing her name slowly, like 'cat-are-zhee-na'. "She's from Poland, she's staying with us for the summer, and she's having a wonderful time, aren't you, Kate?"

Kate nodded. "It's nice to meet you all. I hope I won't be imposing if I accompany you on your sightseeing."

Christina was surprised. She hadn't heard about this! She looked up at Mimi, who read the question on her face.

"Surprise, Christina!" Mimi said, with a sly smile. "You planned our trip so well that I just had to throw in a surprise!"

"Okay, you guys!" Viviana said. "My brother, Vinny, he's outside in the cab waiting to take you wherever you can take a cab. I've got to get back to our new restaurant near Central Park North! Lunchtime starts real soon—say, are you guys hungry? I can call ahead and have Paolo set a table and have today's special waiting for us when we get there. I'm going to call him. You got all your bags? Okay, follow me!"

And just like that, Viviana whirled and made her way

Ben's Mom

Off And Running

to the exit. She whipped out her cell phone and called her restaurant, speaking loudly in Italian.

Christina, Grant, Ben, Kate, and Mimi followed her to the exit. Papa, pushing the luggage cart, huffed behind them. Christina wondered if Viviana's brother Vinny was as colorful a character as she was.

Outside, it *was* quieter. The sounds changed from those of humans to those of vehicles. A big yellow taxivan was waiting for them. As they approached, the sliding door on the side opened automatically. Uncle Vinny came around the back to introduce himself and to help Papa load their bags.

Vinny didn't say much. Christina thought that maybe it was because his sister got all the talking genes. She grabbed her small suitcase from the luggage cart and handed it to him. He just smiled and said, "Buongiorno, signorina!"

Christina went to get into the van and saw Grant standing there with a silly look on his face. "What is it, Grant?"

Grant pointed at the van. "It's a mystery van!" he blurted. "Cool!" On the van's door was an advertisement for the Broadway show *Phantom of the Opera*. It was a spooky-looking banner featuring the famous half-face mask

Off And Running

Meeting Uncle Vinny

and shadowy silhouettes of the characters.

Christina rolled her eyes. She wasn't planning on a being involved in a mystery—they had so much to do, so much to see! She took Grant's hand and led him into the van. They took the second row seats. Viviana was sitting up front, still talking to Paolo on the phone.

"Wow!" Grant exclaimed. "Check it out, Christina!"

Christina looked at him—Grant was staring up at the van's roof. Christina followed his gaze—and looked up and up and up! The roof of the van was one huge window!

Ben and Kate got in and took the seats behind Christina and Grant.

"What a view, eh?" Ben said. "Just wait till we get into the city! You'll think the skyscrapers never end!"

Papa helped Mimi up into the van and they went straight to the back. Vinny closed the sliding door and it got real quiet in the van.

"Okay, you guys," Viviana said, "we're heading to the restaurant! We'll be there in about 20 minutes. Paolo is going to have lunch on the table when we get there!"

Christina's tummy rumbled. It had been a long time since breakfast—and the airlines didn't give you snacks anymore. "What's for lunch, Miss Viviana?" she asked.

Viviana started to reply, but Vinny interrupted her.

Meet Uncle Vinny

What A View!

"Ah! Lunch! My favorite meal of the day!" Vinny proclaimed. "Today, for lunch, we are having *agnello all'aceto balsamico e bocconnoti!*" He turned in his seat and smiled hungrily at them. "I can already smell it!" He took a big sniff, and let it out. "Ahhh!"

"What's that?" Grant asked.

"Lamb with balsamic vinegar and pastries filled with ricotta cheese," Viviana translated.

"Mmmmm!" Papa rumbled from the back seat.

Grant scrunched his eyebrows. "Can I just have plain old spaghetti?"

What A View!

Thinking Of Lunch!

4 WILD RIDE #1

"I ate too much," Grant moaned. "Waaay too much!"

"Me too," Christina groaned. "Waaay too much!"

"I could always eat more!" Vinny said happily as he drove them down Fifth Avenue toward Battery Park, at the southernmost tip of Manhattan. There they would get on the ferry to Liberty Island.

Christina was slumped down in her seat—it made her tummy feel less full, and she was able to look up at the buildings without craning her neck. She and Grant stared up at the skyline-dominating skyscrapers. Their architectural details were fascinating.

"Gargoyle!" Grant shouted every few minutes, pointing wildly at the buildings.

Ben pointed out landmarks as they made their way

To Battery Park

New York Landmarks

through the Upper East Side. "Oh, look! On the left is the Guggenheim Museum!"

"Designed by Frank Lloyd Wright in the 1940s," Christina reported, as they drove by the concrete spiral. "He was one of America's greatest architects!"

Further along, Ben pointed eagerly at a monstrous columned structure. It seemed to stretch for blocks along the tree-lined side of Fifth Avenue. "That's the 'Met', the Metropolitan Museum of Art," he said.

"We're going there!" Grant said. "When are we going?" he asked Christina.

"Tomorrow," Christina replied. "It has the most comprehensive collection of art and antiquities in the Western world! We could spend *days* in there!"

"I *have* spent days in there," Kate said. "Three. It was the first place I went when I arrived in New York. Ben is a very good guide!"

Ben blushed. Christina, peering over the back of her seat, snickered at Ben's slight embarrassment. They rode in silence for a while until they were past Central Park and had crossed through the big intersection at 57th Street.

"Okay," Ben the Tour Guide began, "coming up on the right is Rockefeller Center, built by John D. Rockefeller Jr. and his family, who owned Standard Oil. The land used

New York
Landmarks

Past Central
Park

to be a botanical garden. Rockefeller bought it and was going to build an opera house. But then the Great Depression started, and in a strange twist of fate, some of the largest buildings in the world were constructed instead!"

"Across from it on the left, between 51st and 50th Streets is—" he stopped short as the van came to a screeching halt behind a delivery truck! Grant and Christina almost slid right under their seat belts and off their seats!

"—St. Patrick's Cathedral," Ben finished. "Hey, Vinny! What's going on?"

Vinny thrust a hand toward the windshield. "Ah! Delivery trucks at Rockefeller, maybe, I don't know. I can't see! Is everyone okay?"

Everyone was shaken but okay.

"We're in the middle of the intersection, Vinny," Ben said, a little nervously. "And our traffic light is red!"

"I know! I know!" Vinny replied. "What do you want me to do?"

Suddenly, Grant let out a shriek! "PAPA!" he screamed.

Christina looked past Grant out the left side of the van to see a huge truck barreling right at them!

Past Central Park

AAAHHHH!

"AAAAAAAAAHHHHHH!!!!" Grant screamed as the truck got closer and closer. Christina pulled Grant away from the window as far as the seat belt would allow.

The truck bounced up and down as its driver tried to make the truck stop before it crushed the taxivan—and everyone in it! Christina could see the driver now—both hands gripped the steering wheel, teeth bared and clenched. Smoke streamed from the tires!

"AAAAAAAHHHHHHH!!!!" Grant screamed again.

The truck, just yards away now, was bouncing like crazy! Then it was just feet away! Then inches!

5 WHAT MYSTERY?

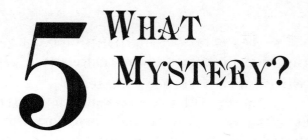

With one final, giant bounce, it stopped! The loud hiss of air brakes releasing pressure and the grumbling engine made it seem like a huge metal monster named MACK.

"AAAAA—" Grant began to scream before Christina clamped a hand over his mouth. "Aaaaahhhhh . . ." Grant's scream faded under his sister's clammy palm.

Vinny looked back at his passengers to see them all as pale as flour, mouths hanging open as if they were moaning like ghosts. Then the "New Yorker" in him took over and he threw open his door. He stood in the open door and cursed in both English and Italian at the truck driver, who promptly returned his own curses.

Christina moved her hands from Grant's mouth and put them on his ears. She didn't want him to hear all those

AAAAAAAAHH
HHHHHHH!

@#%#@****!
*8#&#%!

23

bad words—he probably had heard too many at school as it was! Ben reached forward and covered Christina's ears. Kate listened intently.

Finally, with one last verbal blow at the truck driver, Vinny closed the door and drove forward as the traffic started moving again. Nobody said anything. Christina leaned back in her seat and watched the tall spires of St. Patrick's Cathedral—the largest Catholic church in the United States—slide past.

"Um," Ben said, "if you look to your right between these two buildings—the British Empire Building and La Maison Française—you'll see Rockefeller Plaza, where they have the ice skating rink and the famous Christmas tree."

Everyone looked, but since it was the end of June, there was no Christmas tree. The plaza was full of outdoor cafés and restaurants. Christina thought that the massive G.E. Building was certainly awe-inspiring.

They continued down Fifth Avenue. They all were still in mild shock—mostly from Grant's screaming—over the incident with the truck so Ben was doing his best to keep them entertained.

"Okay," he said, "We're going to cross 42nd Street up ahead. If you look to your left a few block down, you'll see–"

@#%#@****!
*$#&#%!

Still In
Shock

"The Chrysler Building!" Christina interrupted. She was getting back into her comfort zone. "That's my favorite. I like the Art Deco arches."

"Me too," said Grant. After a pause he added, "Who's Art Deco?"

That got everybody back in the laughing mood! Suddenly everyone, even Vinny, was telling Grant what Art Deco was. Grant tried to listen to each person's definition, but Christina saw that he was just getting more and more confused.

"Okay, I get it," he finally said. Christina knew he didn't—but she would try to tell him later.

"Hey, guys!" Ben said. "Look what's up ahead!"

Christina followed Ben's extended arm to a point in the sky where a majestic spire peeked through the surrounding skyscrapers.

"The Empire State Building!" Grant exclaimed. "Where's King Kong?!" Grant pounded his chest and made loud gorilla sounds.

As they drove past the Eighth Wonder of the World, Papa took pictures with his newfangled digital camera. "These will come in handy for that mystery you're writing," he said to Mimi.

"A mystery?!" Kate asked, turning to Mimi and

Still In Shock

Empire State Building

Papa. "What will your mystery be about?"

"Well," Mimi said hesitantly, "it's going to be about the Statue of Liberty, mostly. But I can't tell you much more than that." She leaned forward and whispered, "it would spoil the surprise!"

Up ahead, the taxivan turned off Fifth Avenue onto Broadway.

"Look at that funny building," Grant said, pointing to a triangular-shaped structure jutting out into the intersection.

"That's the Flatiron Building," Christina said. "It was one of the city's first real skyscrapers."

"It was completed in 1902," Kate chimed in. "My great-great grandfather helped build it."

"That's neat!" Christina said. "You have a *real* link to the history of New York!"

In the back of the van, Papa chuckled.

"What are you laughing at, Papa?" Christina asked.

"Twenty-three-skidoo!" Papa said, still chuckling. Mimi rolled her eyes. Christina waited for an explanation.

"It was something the policemen used to say to the men who would gather on 23rd Street," Ben explained. "Back in the early 1900s, women wore long dresses. The wind blows quickly around the Flatiron Building . . ."

Empire State
Building

On
Broadway!

". . . and their dresses would blow up!" Christina finished.

Ben cheerfully continued his tour guide role as they drove down Broadway. There was so much to see, Christina thought. And it's taking forever to get to the ferry! Even Grant started to fidget in his seat.

At one point, Ben excitedly pointed down a bustling cross street. "That's Spring Street," he explained. "Head down that way and you'll be in Little Italy! That's where we live! Later, we'll go have dinner at my Mom's family's *original* restaurant. It's been there for almost 70 years!"

Ben had been telling them why he knew so much about New York City: he often rode with Vinny to give tourists a break from—well, from Vinny. When he realized where they were, Ben told Vinny to go through the next two intersections slowly.

"Everybody look to their right," Ben said in a somber tone. "That's where the World Trade Center used to stand."

Christina's heart sank as she recalled the events of September 11, 2001, when terrorists crashed two jet airplanes into the Twin Towers, eventually causing them to

On Broadway!

Remembering 9/11

collapse to the ground, killing thousands of people. As she gazed down the side streets, she saw the enormous open space in the otherwise crammed-full-of-buildings city. She blinked back a tear and looked away as their view was obscured by the next block of buildings.

"Battery Park is just ahead!" said Vinny.

"Yay!" Christina shouted.

"That was a long ride!" said Papa.

"I gotta go to the bathroom," said Grant.

Remembering
9/11

Battery Park

6 A MIGHTY WOMAN WITH A TORCH

Grant and Christina raced up the stairs to the upper deck of the ferry. Ben and Kate were hot on their heels.

Grant charged to the port side of the ferry and skidded into a seat. A second later, he was back up and hopping around, rubbing the backs of his legs.

"Ow! Ow! Owowowow! That seat's hot!" he cried. Christina beckoned him to the right side—the starboard side—of the ferry.

"Ben says that we want to sit on this side of the boat so we can get a really good view of the Statue of Liberty as we get closer to the island," she explained.

A few minutes later, Mimi and Papa came up and sat with them in the bright early afternoon sunshine. Shortly after that, the ferry began its journey across New York Harbor to Liberty Island.

On The Ferry

Hot Seat!

There were a lot of people on the ferry, but it was not packed full of passengers, like Christina thought it would have been. She reasoned that since it was just the beginning of 4th of July week, the vacationers wouldn't be here yet. She also knew that because the Statue of Liberty was pretty much closed to the public after 9/11, interest in touring the island was down.

Mimi had contacted her congressman and asked if he could get them special permission to tour the statue so she could conduct her research. After all, she was the CEO of her own publishing company, *and* she was writing a kids' mystery book about Lady Liberty! The congressman had personally called her back and said that it was all taken care of. Christina suspected that Mimi had offered him an autographed copy of the mystery when it was finally published.

The ride was very pleasant. There was just a little breeze coming in off the ocean, and the water seemed as smooth as glass. Christina saw small sailboats plying the water close to shore and gigantic freighters navigating the deeper waters of the Hudson River.

Long before they arrived at the island, they could

Hot Seat!

To Liberty Island

see the silhouette of the Statue of Liberty through the light haze that blanketed the harbor. The sight of her standing, it seemed, in the middle of the water, transfixed everybody on board.

As they drew closer, the haze faded and the gray silhouette brightened to reveal the greenish color of the Lady's "skin." The sun glinted off the torch and sparkled in everyone's eyes. Christina looked down and saw the statue's reflection reaching out across the water towards the ferry.

"Gosh," Grant said, "how long did it take to paint that statue?"

"That's not paint, Grant," Papa replied. "It's a *patina*."

"A what? Paint Tina?" Grant said.

"*Patina*. It's caused by oxidation," Ben explained. "It's what happens when oxygen in the air reacts with the copper skin."

"It's **corrosion**, right?" Christina said. "Kind of like rust on iron."

"Right," Ben said. "It's just prettier than rust!"

At last, the ferry docked at the pier. Christina couldn't wait to get off the boat and onto the island! After the boat docked, they began the long wait to disembark.

To Liberty Island

Docking At The Pier

That's one drawback to sitting on the top deck, Christina thought. She thought about how impatient and excited the early immigrants to the New World must have felt waiting to set foot in their new homeland. Finally, at long last, Christina, Grant, and the rest of the entourage stepped onto Liberty Island!

Docking At
The Pier

To The Statue
Of Liberty!

Look! There's the statue!

7 MOTHER OF EXILES

"All right, kids," Mimi said, "let's get to the statue! You walk around outside and take pictures while I find our tour guide."

They strolled past a concession stand and information center and onto a large, round, brick-paved patio. They turned, and ahead of them, down a long, wide walkway, was the Lady herself! They all stopped and gazed in amazement for a minute. Grant wiped a film of perspiration off his forehead.

"Whew! It's hot out here!" he complained. "We *are* going inside the statue, right? It's gotta be cooler in there."

"It should be," Mimi said.

"Cool!" Grant took the lead to the statue's entrance.

Mimi went inside to find the tour guide. Papa and

To The Statue
Of Liberty!

Waiting for
Our Tour

the kids walked around the statue and took pictures. The Lady was enormous! To stand at her feet and gaze up was to behold a giant worthy of legend.

To Christina's annoyance, she heard Grant mutter, "It's the jolly green giant!"

"Don't be disrespectful!" his sister warned him.

Finally, Mimi returned with a tall, elderly black man, dressed in a Park Ranger uniform, in tow.

"Christina! Grant! Ben! Kate!" she said. "This is Franklin. He's going to give us the tour today. Are you ready?"

"YEEESSS!!" they all shouted. They followed Franklin to the entrance of the museum where a security guard scanned them. Once they were all cleared, they stepped through the doors and into the cool air of the old fortress upon which the statue was erected.

Christina led the way. The magnificent centerpiece of the museum was what she thought was the *original* iron-and-glass torch. **Corrosion** from 100 years of exposure to the wind, rain, sun, snow, hail, and birds had rusted the metal and eaten away at the nuts and bolts holding it together. An odd framework of support beams surrounded the torch.

"What are they doing to the original torch, Mr.

Waiting for
Our Tour

An Old
Torch

Franklin?" Christina asked.

"Please, please," Franklin said in a low, soothing voice, "call me Franklin. No Mister. Just Franklin."

He gazed fondly at the torch. "We're having it taken off the island for refurbishment—and duplication. We want to have it repaired so that when the statue and museum finally reopen to the public, it can be a star attraction."

"Why can't you repair it here?" Ben asked. "And when will the statue reopen?"

"Two good questions," Franklin commended. "First, some of the equipment needed for the refurbishment can't be brought to the island. Second . . . I just don't know."

"So you're making a copy of it?" Christina asked.

"Right again," Franklin said. "Eventual plans are to replace the 1986 gold-plated torch with an exact replica of this *second* torch."

"*Second* torch?" Christina was confused. "This isn't the original?"

"No, ma'am," Franklin said. "The first torch our Lady held was made of copper. It corroded too quickly in the salty air and became dangerously unstable high up at the end of the Lady's arm. It was replaced in 1916 with this one. This one was designed by Gutzon Borglum, the famous sculptor who created a national monument at

An Old Torch

Taking It Off
The Island

Mount Rushmore."

"Oh, yeah!" Grant said. "That mountain in South Dakota with the four dudes carved on it!"

"Those aren't *four dudes*, Grant! Those are some of the most important presidents America ever had!" Christina exclaimed.

"Yeah, yeah . . . let's start the tour!" Grant said.

Their tour began with a ride in an elevator to the top of the **pedestal** upon which Lady Liberty stood. As they walked around the observation area, Franklin told them about the statue.

"At 151 feet tall and 225 tons, the Statue of Liberty was first delivered *completely constructed* to the American Ambassador in Paris, France. The largest metal statue ever made, she towered 15 stories over the streets of Paris, where the tallest buildings were, at that time, only four or five stories high.

"French sculptor Frédéric-Auguste Bartholdi designed the statue's exterior, or skin, if you will. Wooden frames were constructed, upon which sheets of copper— only 3/32nd of an inch thick—were molded into shape.

"The statue was supposed to be delivered in time

Taking It Off
The Island

Lady Liberty
Tour

for America's Centennial in 1876. But, here in America, coming up with enough money to complete the pedestal upon which the statue would stand was tough. About $179,000 was spent for the construction, then the money ran out. Joseph Pulitzer, the man behind the famous Pulitzer Prize, led an effort to get enough money to finish the pedestal."

"Who paid for the statue?" Christina asked. "It must have cost a lot!"

"The French paid for the statue," Franklin answered. "It was actually a gift from the French people to America."

Franklin asked the group, "Does anyone know who designed the statue's supporting framework?"

"Gustave Eiffel!" Christina reported. "He also built the Eiffel Tower in Paris."

"That's right," Franklin said. "We'll get a look at the framework as we climb the 168 stairs to the top of the statue." He led them up the long, narrow, twisty spiral staircase and continued his lecture as he walked.

Christina tried to focus on the intricate spider web of beams, girders, straps, and guy wires, but it proved to be too confusing!

"In order to get the statue to New York," Franklin

Lady Liberty
Tour

Gift from
The French

said, "it had to be dismantled. The colossal statue was reduced to 350 meticulously labeled and diagrammed pieces, which were packed into 214 specially constructed crates. The crates were loaded onto a French frigate, the *Isere*, and brought here, to what was then called Bedloe's Island."

Christina's mind wandered off into a daydream about the statue's long journey across the Atlantic Ocean. She heard Mimi peppering Franklin with questions as they climbed the stairs to the Lady's crown. She also heard Papa telling Grant to stop monkeying around on the stairs. But it was all just background noise in her daydream of burly sailors, sailing ships, and throngs of people waving handkerchiefs and shouting *au revoir!* as the ship left for America.

When she came back to the present, the tour group was standing at the windows in the statue's crown. The view was spectacular! Out loud, Grant counted 25 windows, through which they could see Manhattan, the Brooklyn Bridge, Governor's Island, and out, out, out to the Atlantic Ocean!

They posed for pictures while Franklin went on divulging everything he knew about the Statue of Liberty.

"Let's continue our tour," Franklin finally said.

Gift from The french

Crown Windows

"We'll go back downstairs and take a walk through the pedestal."

As they made their way back downstairs, Grant noticed a door. "Where's that door go?" Grant asked.

"That leads to a ladder that travels up the arm to the torch," Franklin said.

"Can we go up there?!" Grant pleaded. "Please?!"

Franklin laughed. "No, no, no. It's not safe. Besides, only the maintenance crew has the keys."

"Phooey!" Grant pouted.

Once they were back at the top level of the pedestal, Mimi and Franklin went off on their own. So they could discuss mystery stuff, Christina thought as she looked around. She saw that there were green glass-like plaques mounted on the walls of the pedestal. She walked over to one and read it.

"I would rather belong to a poor nation that was free than to a rich nation that had ceased to be in love with liberty. —Franklin D. Roosevelt."

Christina pondered that and decided that President Roosevelt 'hit that nail on the head', as Papa would say.

She read the other plaques, too. They were all statements made by famous Americans, except for one that came from the Bible's Old Testament.

Crown
Windows

Famous
Quotes

Mimi and Franklin came back from their private conversation, and they all walked down to another level of the pedestal. Christina saw that there were more plaques on the walls, and as she read them, Papa took pictures. These were actually the dedication tablets from the Franco-American Union—the donor of the statue—and the American Committee, which had erected the pedestal.

Franklin went off somewhere and reappeared with a small stack of books. "Kids, these are for you," he said. "They're the latest edition of the official guide to the Statue of Liberty, and you are the first four people to get one!"

He handed one each to Christina, Grant, Ben, and Kate. They were hardbound, faux-leather-wrapped books with *Liberty Enlightening the World* stamped in gold on the cover.

"Wow! These are neat! Thank you, Franklin!" Christina said.

"Yeah, thanks, Franklin!" Grant echoed.

"*Dziekuja*," said Kate in her native tongue.

"*A dank aych*," said Ben.

"Wow! A multicultural group!" Franklin said. "I think I heard Polish and Yiddish, there."

Ben and Kate nodded, obviously pleased that he

famous Quotes

Official
Statue Guide

recognized their languages.

"Great! Well, let's get back to the entrance. I have another private tour due in about ten minutes." As he led them out of the pedestal, he said, "I hope you've enjoyed your tour!"

"Yes, sir, we have!" said Christina. "I hope the statue reopens soon so that everyone else can see what we've seen today."

"You and me both!" Franklin said wishfully. "It gets lonely in here sometimes!"

As the group passed the old torch, Christina saw that it was already suspended from the framework that would carry it to the wherever it was being taken. Three men in grubby uniforms were checking to make sure it would travel well.

As the tour group made their way out, Christina's backpack shifted and it fell off her shoulder, spilling some of its contents across the floor. "Oh, poo!" she said, bending down to recover the items. Christina heard the men working with the torch talking. . .

"Hey, this is gonna be easier than I thought!" one said.

"No kiddin'! Nobody suspects a thing!" another replied.

Official Statue
Guide

Oh, Poo!

"This 'refurbishment' deal is the best cover! I don't think I coulda thought of it!" the first said.

"I don't think youz guys could think of anything this complicated by yourself!" a third voice said.

"Yeah, yeah. . . whadda you know?" said the second.

"I'm the one who thought of this plan!" the third said.

"Christina! Let's go!" Papa called.

Christina hesitated. What the workmen said sounded suspicious—maybe even dangerous. But maybe they were just grouchy from having to work in that tight squeeze of a place.

Once outside, as she left the fortress walls behind, Christina noticed that the sun had moved far across the sky since they had begun their tour. She looked at her Carole Marsh Mysteries watch—they had been touring for nearly three hours!

"Look!" Grant said, pointing to the ferry nearing the dock.

"If we hurry, we can catch that ferry and see some of Ellis Island before it closes," Christina said.

"All right!" Mimi said. "Then let's hurry! I'm still in search of a mystery!"

Oh, Poo!

To Ellis Island!

8 A MYSTERIOUS PUZZLE

Back on the ferry, Christina led her group to a row of seats on the lowest deck. Out on the water, she saw a white boat that looked like a miniature freighter heading toward Liberty Island. A small crane sprouted from the stern and leaned over the main deck. That must be the boat coming to get the torch, Christina thought.

Grant plopped down and picked up the newspaper that was on the empty seat next to his. "Where are the funnies. . . where are the funnies. . ." he muttered, shuffling through pages.

Christina settled into her seat and opened the handsome book Franklin had given her. The binding made a creaky crackling sound as it was opened for the first time. She pressed her nose to the pages and sniffed. She adored the smell of fresh, new books—hot off the press.

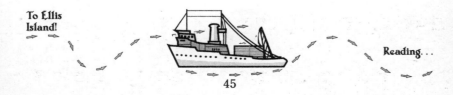

To Ellis Island!

Reading. . .

45

She flipped past the introduction and table of contents, then the foreword, and all the other front matter to the "meat" of the book. She flipped and flipped past all the text until she got to a set of "plates"—pages made of paper thicker and glossier than the rest of the book. The plates were reserved for photographs. And there were a LOT of photographs, mostly real old ones.

Christina spent the short trip to Ellis Island studying the old-timey photos. She heard Ben and Kate behind her, talking about their books. Grant giggled as he read the funnies.

One particular picture captured Christina's attention. "Hey, guys," she said, turning around to Ben and Kate. "Did you know that the Statue of Liberty has broken shackles around her feet?"

"It does?" said Kate, surprised. She and Ben studied the photograph.

"The statue *is* a symbol of freedom," Mimi said.

"Attention, ladies and gentlemen!" a voice blared over the ferry's public address system. "We are now preparing to dock at Ellis Island. Please ready all of your belongings and make sure you have your immigration papers ready for inspection!"

Many of the passengers on the ferry chuckled. No

Reading. . .

Ready To
Dock

one on *this* boat needs immigration papers, Christina thought. She closed her book and tucked it into her backpack. Grant folded the newspaper and tucked it under his arm with his book.

"Why don't you leave that paper for someone else, Grant?" Christina suggested.

"'Cause I'm not done reading it, yet, Christina," he retorted. "I want to look at it some more."

"Whatever," Christina sighed.

As Christina stepped off the ramp onto Ellis Island, she felt an inkling of what it might have been like a hundred years ago—to be one of 23 million immigrants stepping off a crowded steamship onto the soil of a strange country, with few possessions, sometimes very little money, and no idea of what lay ahead.

What *was* it like, Christina thought, to be drawn to these shores by the dreams of plenty of work, abundant food and housing, and promises of quick riches? Most everyone who came here did not see those dreams come true—if they didn't return home out of despair, they spent the rest of their lives working their fingers to the bone for the basics needed for survival. But some prospered beyond

Ready To Dock

Ellis Island

their wildest dreams, to become millionaires and tycoons!

"Edward stood right here when he came to America," Kate said reverently. "I can imagine the wonder he felt when he arrived."

"Your great-great-grandfather?" Christina asked.

Kate nodded and said, "I have a diary that he kept from the time he began making plans to come to America until his children were in school."

"Wow! What is it like?" Christina was *very* intrigued.

"Hmm. . . there was a lot of. . . excitement about he and his new wife, Stella, coming to America. . . and a lot of sadness. They were leaving behind their homes and families," Kate explained, as they walked under a long metal and glass awning toward the main building.

"What was the trip like?" Ben asked. "When did he come?"

"What kind of boat was it?" Grant wanted to know.

Kate thought about it. "The boat was a steamship. He and Stella arrived here in 1897. They were fortunate that they had enough money to afford the higher fares that allowed them to make the passage on one of the upper decks."

"Why is that fortunate?" Christina asked.

"Because," Kate replied, "the lower fares were for

Ellis Island

Across The
Ocean

passage in the 'steerage' section of the ships—the section meant for transporting cargo and animals."

Christina and Grant scrunched up their noses. Ben made a gagging noise. By now, they were walking through the Great Hall, where immigrants once had to wait to be "processed" in the Registry Room.

"That is what it was like!" Kate said. "Those poor passengers could not go to the upper decks and get fresh air. They were locked down there like animals! Edward wrote that the people who went down there at the beginning of the voyage were not the same when they came up at the end. They had little food, barely drinkable water, no sunlight, and hardly any room to move around for two weeks!"

"That's terrible!" Christina exclaimed.

"Icky!" said Grant.

"Edward also wrote that many of the people who were on the lower decks on his voyage were **quarantined** on this island because they were sick. Most of them had gotten *trachoma*, a disease that causes blindness, and there was no medicine to treat it."

"Gosh!" Christina said.

"But that was not the end of it," Kate continued. "Sometimes there were so many immigrants waiting to

Across The
Ocean

Poor
Conditions

enter the United States that there was no room on the
island for them. They had to wait on the ships."

By now, they were walking around the top of the
Great Hall. They passed through the Dormitory, where
detained passengers were kept until they were set free in
America or told that they had to return home.

"There was one real neat thing about the voyage,
though," Kate said. "The balls of yarn."

"Balls of yarn?" Grant repeated.

"Balls of yarn," Kate said again. "When Edward and
Stella came to America, they each brought a ball of yarn—
and so did many other passengers. Family members
standing on the docks held the loose ends, and as the ship
left port, the yarn unraveled. When it was completely
unwound, there were long streamers trailing behind the
ship for miles!"

"Wow! That's cool!" Grant said. "I'm gonna try that
if we ever go on a cruise!"

"Umm. . . so why are you from Poland?" Christina
asked. "Didn't your great-great-grandfather stay here?"

"He established a family and a successful business
here in America," Kate explained. "Some of the family
went back to Poland after World War II to help rebuild the
country. My father went back in 1990 to help rebuild again

Poor
Conditions

Balls Of
Yarn?

after the communist government was replaced by a democratic government. That is when he met my mother."

"Are you planning on coming to America to live?" Ben asked. "Part of your family is still here, right?"

"No, I do not think we will be immigrating to America," Kate smiled at him. "Poland is such a beautiful country with such rich culture and history. And yes, we still have family in America, but we have lost touch with many of them as the family grows. While I am here, one of my goals is to try to contact as many of them as I can."

"That's so neat!" Christina said. "You being here made this experience so much more authentic!" Kate blushed and smiled.

They had reached the end of their tour of Ellis Island. It was time to catch the next ferry back to Manhattan. Christina ducked into the gift shop and bought a book about Ellis Island and another about immigration. Mimi was *very* happy about that!

Grant yawned as they waited for the ferry to arrive. "It's been a *loooong* day!" he said, stating the obvious. He leaned against Papa's leg.

"Just one more ferry ride," Papa said, "and one more ride in the taxivan, and we'll be done for the day, Grant."

Balls Of
Yarn?

Long Day!

As they rode the ferry back to Manhattan, Christina stood near the windows on the starboard side of the boat. She could see the Statue of Liberty. She also saw the white mini-freighter plying its way from Liberty Island to Manhattan. She could see a large crate on its deck—the torch! It was going much faster than the ferry, and it was soon far ahead of them, heading up the East River.

"Hey, Christina!" she heard Grant call out. He was walking toward her with the newspaper in hand. He held it up. Christina saw that he had carefully folded the paper so that it showed half of one particular page.

"Look at this weird puzzle I found!"

Always a sucker for a good puzzle, Christina looked at the paper. She read the puzzle. And read it again. It was a riddle *and* a puzzle!

"Wow! This *is* weird, Grant!" she said. "I wonder what this means!"

The jailed lightning shall be set free
Off the shores of here, 'tis of thee.

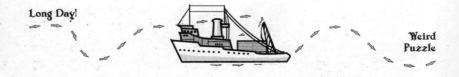

Long Day!

Weird Puzzle

Since wretched refuse has been refused
And the lady's lamp all but used
A flame extinguished, to light no more;
Lost forever from this teeming shore.
By the rockets' red glare, seek the crate
Or the sea shall wash the light from the sunset-gate.

Directly below this curious passage was a jumble puzzle:

The Game's Afoot!

Fill in the blanks to match the clues.
Unscramble the mystery words.
The topic is: Enlightening the World

__ windows on the world
Passage to the New World __
He gets the prize for finance __
The Lady has broken her __
Freedom's light redesigned, by __

Weird Puzzle

NEWS!

The Game's Afoot!

9 WILD RIDE #2

"This is *weird*, Grant!" Christina repeated. "How did you find this?"

Grant shrugged his shoulders. "It just kinda jumped out at me. The words looked familiar, I guess."

Christina looked around. There was no one within hearing distance. Ben, Kate, Mimi, and Papa were sitting about twenty or so rows ahead of where she and Grant were standing.

"Where have I seen this before?" Christina said, frustrated with herself for not remembering. It had been a very long day, and she was tired.

"Attention, ladies and gentlemen!" said the voice from the speakers. "We are preparing to dock at Battery Park. We hope you have enjoyed your visits to Liberty and Ellis Islands. From the crew of the Circle Line Ferry and

How Did You
Find This?

Back To
Battery Park

on behalf of the staff at Liberty and Ellis Islands, we thank you!"

Just minutes later, as they trotted down the ramp to the dock, Christina was practically pounding her forehead as she tried to remember why those words were so familiar!

Ben took out his cell phone and called Vinny to tell them they were back in Manhattan and ready to be picked up.

Grant looked at Christina with a serious expression. "It has something to do with the Statue of Liberty, doesn't it?" he asked in a whisper. "Do you think something's going to happen to it?"

"Something may have *already* happened, Grant," Christina whispered back.

"*What* happened?" Ben whispered.

Christina jumped, not expecting Ben to be whispering in her ear. "Ahh! You scared me!" she said. "I think something may have happened to the Statue of Liberty!"

"What?" Kate asked.

Christina looked back at Mimi and Papa. They were a good distance back, unable to hear them talking. "Grant," she said, "show them the newspaper."

Back To
Battery Park

Calling
Vinny

We're back in Manhattan!

Ben and Kate read the riddle and the puzzle.

Kate shook her head. She had no idea.

But Ben, Mister New York Tour Guide, had an idea. "It's a poem," he remembered, "that sounds like the one written about the statue."

"THAT'S IT!" Christina shouted. "Oops!" she said, as she glanced back at Mimi and Papa, who *were* looking at them now. Christina smiled and waved at them as she got her Statue of Liberty guidebook out of her backpack.

"Here it is!" she exclaimed. "Listen to this:

Not like the brazen giant of Greek fame,
With conquering limbs astride from land to land;
Here at our sea-washed, sunset gates shall stand
A Mighty Woman with a torch, whose flame
Is the imprisoned lightning, and her name
Mother of Exiles. From her beacon hand
Glows world-wide welcome; her mild eyes command
The air-bridged harbor that twin cities frame.
"Keep, ancient lands, your storied pomp!" cries she,
With silent lips. "Give me your tired, your poor,
Your huddled masses yearning to breathe free,
The wretched refuse of your teeming shore;
Send these, the homeless, tempest-tost to me,

Calling Yinny

NEWS!

Look At This!

I lift my lamp beside the golden door!"

"Emma Lazarus, November 2, 1883," Christina finished.

"We need to solve the riddle!" Grant exclaimed.

A honking horn startled them from the mysterious clues. Vinny's taxivan was just ahead.

"We'll have to save this for later," Christina said, "when we don't have *adults* around." She stuffed her book and the newspaper into her backpack.

"But do you not think that this is important?" Kate asked.

"I do, Kate," Christina replied, "but then, this *could* be a hoax, or just a trick of some kind. I just don't know!"

"Buona sera!" Vinny greeted them as they reached the taxivan. "Did you have a good trip? The Lady was quite enchanting, no?"

"Why does he say 'no' when he means 'yes'?" Grant asked his sister. But Christina just pushed him into the van.

"You have come back at rush hour," Vinny said. "There is a lot of traffic, now. But you don't worry, no? I can get us to Little Italy in no time!"

Look At This!

Off To Little Italy!

With that, he launched the van into a gap in the traffic. The sudden turn nearly lifted the van's right side off the street. The van surged ahead, its engine roaring like a racecar. Christina buried her fingers in the armrests. Grant let out a "Wheeee!" Mimi clutched her seatbelt, and Papa wiped his brow.

Ben chuckled. "Vinny only drives like this when he's hungry," he informed the group.

"Sì!" Vinny said. "It is time for dinner! And dinner is my favorite meal!"

"I thought lunch was your favorite meal," Grant said.

"It is! But so is dinner!"

"And breakfast," Ben added. "Okay, tour guide time! We're heading up South Street. Up ahead is the famous Fulton Street Fish Market. The site was developed in 1814 by Robert Fulton—"

"—inventor of the steamboat!" Grant chimed in.

"Right," Ben said. "It was for his Manhattan-to-Brooklyn ferry. Seafood dealers have been selling their seafood here since 1834."

"Is that the Brooklyn Bridge?" Christina asked, pointing up ahead.

"Sure is!" Ben said. "Did you know that for years,

Off To Little Italy!

Brooklyn Bridge

that 3,580-foot bridge was the longest in the world? When it opened in 1883, it was the first steel suspension bridge."

The van suddenly swerved off South Street and down a side street, narrowly missing a truck and a dumpster. Another tire-screeching turn, then another, and another!

Ben kept offering tidbits of information about the areas they were driving through. He kept them real short, since it seemed everyone was more concerned about Vinny's driving and all the close calls with cars, trucks, and light poles. They didn't slow down until the traffic was bumper-to-bumper as they approached Little Italy.

They turned one last corner, and there, stretched out ahead of them, was one of the streets out onto which Little Italy's restaurants and markets had spilled. This street was normally closed to vehicles, except for special deliveries. Vinny honked the horn as he stopped at a gate-like barricade. A man waved and hurried to move the gate out of the way. He cheerfully waved at Vinny's passengers as the van crept down the street.

People were everywhere, talking, laughing, and shopping for breads, vegetables, meats, and different kinds of delicacies for their dinners. Colorful banners were strung across the streets from building to building. Signs

Brooklyn
Bridge

In Little
Italy!

sprouted from the facades, advertising all sorts of businesses. Colorful awnings sheltered the merchants and their wares.

"This. . . is. . . sooo. . . neat!" Christina said. She had always wanted to visit a cultural community like this. Finally, here she was, in maybe the best one in the world!

Vinny stopped and backed the van into an alley. "We are here! Fast, and in one piece, no?!" He got out and ran around to open the side door.

He held out his hand to help Christina out of the van. With dramatic flair, he bowed and swept his arm toward the bustling street.

"Welcome to my home!"

In Little Italy!   Welcome!

10 The Game's Afoot!

Christina stacked her empty plate atop Grant's to make room for her notebook on the table. At the other end of the long table, the chattering adults ignored them.

"Where do we start?" Christina muttered. "With the riddle," she answered herself.

Grant had to kneel in his seat to see.

"Let's see. . ." Christina began. "*The jailed lightning shall be set free. Jailed* is a synonym for *imprisoned*. And the *imprisoned lightning* in Emma Lazarus' poem is the flame of the torch."

"So the torch is going to be set free?" Grant wondered aloud. "How?"

"Let's find out," Christina said excitedly, continuing the riddle, "*Off the shores* would mean that it's not on land—or won't be when it's set free."

Finishing
Dinner

Work On
The Puzzle

"My country 'tis of thee, sweet land of Liberty. . ." Grant sang.

"America!" Kate said. "I think that means it will be off the shores of America when it is set free."

"So will it be set free in another country?" Ben asked. "Or maybe just dumped in the water? Perhaps near Liberty Island?"

"That's a scary thought!" Christina said. Continuing with the riddle, she read, *"Since wretched refuse has been refused."*

"What's wretched refuse?" Grant asked. "Stinky garbage?"

"No, no, no," Christina objected. "It's people—the tired, the poor, the huddled masses. It's right in the poem."

"Refused. . ." Ben pondered. "Sounds like somebody wasn't allowed to enter the United States."

Christina gasped. "That must be the motive! Somebody *wasn't* allowed to enter, and somebody else got *real* mad about it!"

"Mad enough to steal a huge torch and dump it in the harbor?" Grant said. "That's crazy!"

"Get mad enough and you will do crazy things," Kate offered.

Work On The
Puzzle

Stealing A
Torch?

"I think the next line is just filler," Christina said. "I don't see how it might help. Same for the next two lines. They're just reinforcing the threat of the torch being lost forever."

"And the rockets' red glare, the bombs bursting in air. . ." Grant sang. "Does that mean fireworks?"

"That's good, Grant!" Christina praised. "It does! Fireworks weren't called fireworks back when the *Star-Spangled Banner* was written. They called them rockets."

"The Fourth of July is only three days away!" Ben cried.

"We have to find the crate with the torch in it before the fireworks display on the Fourth of July!" Christina exclaimed.

"Or the sea is going to wash it away from the sunset-gate!" Kate finished.

They all sat wide-eyed at the table in Ben's family's restaurant. Christina felt like the weight of the world was placed on her shoulders. This wasn't just a simple little mystery like they usually got involved in—there was a priceless, irreplaceable piece of history in danger!

"We need to solve the puzzle *now*," Grant said.

"We do! That's the first clue!" Christina said. "Okay, let's do this. The topic is, 'Enlightening the World.'

Stealing A Torch?

On July fourth?

Look at the front of the Statue of Liberty book. It's titled
Liberty Enlightening the World. That's the real name of the
Statue of Liberty."

"Ten blanks," Christina read. "What are the
'Windows on the world'?"

"The windows at the top of the statue?" Kate
offered.

"Yes!" Christina said. "There are 25 windows in the
crown!" She filled in the blanks of the first mystery word.

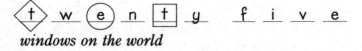

windows on the world

"Five blanks," Christina read. "The statue's
'passage to the New World' was aboard a French ship—the
Isere!" She filled in the blanks of the second mystery word.

Passage to the New World

i s e r e

"Joseph Pulitzer, creator of the Pulitzer Prize, got
the money to pay for the pedestal!" Christina said, her
mind's gears whirring at top speed now.

On July
fourth?

Fill In The
Blanks

Working on the puzzle. . .

Who gets the prize for finance

p (u) l i (t) (z) (e) r

"And the shackles at the statue's feet are broken!" Christina said frantically.

The Lady has broken her

⟨s⟩ h a c k (l) e s

"What was the name of the guy who designed the second torch?" Christina hurriedly asked the group. Ben and Kate lowered their heads in concentration. Grant looked at Christina.

"It was the same guy who made Mount Rushmore," he said helpfully.

"Yeah! But what was his name?" Christina said.

"Look in the book," Grant said.

Christina grabbed the guidebook and scanned the table of contents. "Aha!" she exclaimed, as she turned chunks of pages at a time to get to the page she needed. "Here it is!"

Freedom's light redesigned, by

B o r (g) l u [m]

Fill In The Blanks

About The Statue

"That's it! You did it, Christina!" Kate praised her.

"Now we have to unscramble the letters," Grant moaned.

"I have something that'll help," Ben said. He jumped out of his seat and ran to the back of the restaurant. He returned with a Scrabble box, got out the bag of letters, and dumped the tiles on the table with a clatter.

They sorted out the letters they needed for the big clue and arranged them in rows according to their enclosing shapes.

"The first one's easy!" Grant said, as he rearranged the three tiles to spell:

"I've got the next one!" Christina said. She rearranged the three tiles to spell:

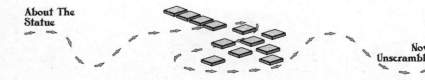

"We're going to the Metropolitan Museum of Art

tomorrow!" Christina said excitedly. Then her eyebrows creased. "But where do we go? That place is huge!"

"The last word might be a room, or a collection," Ben said, "or even just one piece of art."

The tiles on the table looked like this:

Christina sighed and slumped back in her seat. "We have to wait until tomorrow to find out, I guess," she said dejectedly. "I don't think we could find anything at this time of night to help us on this one." She was disappointed. It could take days to find what they were looking for, and they didn't even know what it was!

"Christina?" Grant said. "What about your New York survival guide?"

"Oh!" With all the focus on the Statue of Liberty, she had forgotten all about it—and this particular guide had *everything* in it! "Thanks, Grant!"

She fished in her backpack and brought out the book. She flipped through the pages, following the headers that listed the areas of Manhattan. "Ben! Where's the Met?"

Now
Unscramble

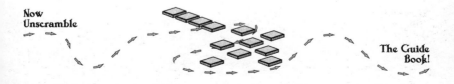

The Guide
Book!

"Um, it's on Fifth Avenue, Central Park East," he replied.

"What area?"

"Uh, that's the Upper East Side."

Christina stopped when she reached the pages that had information about the Met. There were floor plans, pictures of exhibits, color-coded listings of the exhibit areas, and "star exhibits"—the things you *had* to see when you visited.

"I FOUND IT! I FOUND IT!" Christina shouted. She slapped the book down on the table and rearranged the letter tiles to spell:

"What's that?" Grant asked.

"Edward Gottlieb Leutze!" Christina said. "He painted the famous painting of George Washington crossing the Delaware! THAT is where we'll find the next clue!"

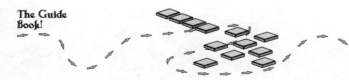

The Guide Book!

To The Met!

11 MEETING OF THE MINDS AT THE MET

When the doors of the Metropolitan Museum of Art opened the next morning, Christina, Grant, Ben, and Kate were the first ones inside. Christina had been surprised that there was no mention of a missing torch in the morning newspapers or on the morning TV news shows.

As Papa paid for their admission, the ticket seller informed him that children MUST be supervised at ALL TIMES, and should be kept IN SIGHT at ALL TIMES.

So the kids had to stick with Mimi and Papa for the whole morning while they wandered through rooms of Greek and Roman art, then a mishmash of "special" collections. Grant was interested by some of the medieval art, but all Christina wanted to do was break away from the adults and run to the museum's collection of American art!

She wished she wasn't so preoccupied with a

To The Met!

Stuck With
Adults

mystery because she really wanted to absorb a lot of the wondrous artwork. But, somehow, fate always threw a twist at her. This time, Christina ended up walking through entire collections of art without really seeing them.

"There it is!" Christina whispered to Grant, as they peeked around a corner into a room-within-a-room.

"The painting!" Grant said. But neither of them moved. Christina was frozen to the spot, afraid that the riddle and puzzle *were* just a hoax, and there was no clue for them to find here.

"Where's the clue?" Grant whispered. "I don't see anything."

"What *is* the clue?" Christina said. "Whatever it is, it's *got* to be here! "Let's go find it!" She grabbed Grant's hand and led him into the room.

"It's huge!" Grant said, looking up at the work of art.

Christina headed for a large tilted information table about the painting. From there, she studied the painting's vast canvas, but saw nothing that shouted, "I'm a clue!"

She scanned the pictures and text on the table for

Stuck With
Adults

There It Is!

anything out of the ordinary that could be a clue.

She shook her head. "I'm not finding anything, Grant. Do you see anything that could be a clue?"

Grant peered at the painting from as close as the velvet ropes would allow. "Nuh-uh," he grunted.

"Grant!" Christina cried, "I need your help!"

Grant turned from the painting and looked at her with an expression of "what do you want *me* to do?" Then, his expression changed. His eyebrows lowered, and he pointed at the table. "Maybe that's a clue," he said.

"What is?" Christina demanded. Grant pointed. Christina came around the table and saw what Grant was pointing to: a little white address label with letters written on it.

"Oh, brother!" Christina said. "What is that supposed to mean?" Grant just shrugged his shoulders.

On the little white address label were these letters:

$$\boxed{\text{DENE WA B}}$$

"Where's Ben?" Grant asked. "Maybe he'll know what 'den-ah-wab' means. He's Mister New York Tour Guide."

There It Is!

A Clue?

"There you are!" Papa's voice startled them. "We thought you might have been captured by the Met police!" Mimi, Ben, and Kate followed Papa into the room.

"Wow! Look at the size of that painting!" Mimi exclaimed. "I didn't know it was so big!" She and Papa made their way to the information table as Christina and Grant walked to the other side of the room.

"Is there a clue?" Ben whispered.

"Yes," Christina whispered back. "It's just a bunch of letters: *D-E-N-E-W-A-B*. Do they mean anything to you?"

Ben considered the cryptic clue. "Well. . ." he thought out loud, "if you ignore the last three letters, you're left with DENE, which is a section of Central Park, near the Zoo."

"Hey, that's a start!" Christina said. "What's there that 'WAB' might stand for?"

Ben shook his head. Kate could offer nothing, since she had never been there.

"Christina. . ." Grant said. "Your survival guide?" he hinted.

Without a word, Christina got the guidebook out of her backpack and flipped through the pages to the section on Central Park. She scanned the pages that featured photographs of the you-gotta-see-these things and maps of

A Clue?

To The Book!

the park. On the very last page, in the very last column, Christina found what she was looking for.

"BALTO!" she cried. "Near Willowdell Arch!"

To The Book!

Balto!

12 A WALK IN THE PARK

After getting lunch from a hot dog and sausage vendor in Central Park, the group meandered toward Willowdell Arch. It was another picture-perfect day, with hardly a cloud in the sky.

Christina felt better than she had this morning—the nervous butterflies in her stomach had apparently flown away. Maybe it was the hot dogs, she wondered. They walked in silence for quite a while, until the trees along the path opened to reveal a calm lake with little model boats cruising about.

"That's Conservatory Water," Ben told them. "It's also called the Model Boat Pond."

"I like model boats," Grant happily chirped.

"Me, too," said Ben. "If we have time on Saturday, we can come back and watch them race!"

In Central Park

To Willowdell Arch

"What's that statue?" Christina asked, pointing to an odd group of bronze figures around what looked like giant mushrooms. She veered off the path and headed for the statue without waiting for the answer.

"It's Alice in Wonderland!" she proclaimed. "There's Alice, the Rabbit, the Mad Hatter, the Dormouse—"

"—and the Cheshire Cat!" Grant added. "Meow!" He smiled as widely as he could and walked around saying, "Meow!" Christina rolled her eyes, but she smiled at her brother's silly antics.

"Look at the Mad Hatter," Ben said. "That's a caricature of George T. Delacorte. He was a publisher and a **philanthropist**. He had this statue created in honor of his wife."

"Delacorte Theater is where they perform Shakespeare in the Park," Mimi added.

Papa took a picture as Grant—still smiling and meowing—got up on Alice's toadstool and slid down it.

"Okay, let's keep going!" Christina commanded, and set off back to the path.

Further around the pond, she spied another statue, this one of a man sitting on a park bench. Again Christina made a detour and headed for the statue.

To Willowdell Arch

Statues!

"Hans Christian Andersen and the Ugly Duckling," she read from an inscription. She sat down next to Hans and pulled Grant next to her. "Take a picture, Papa!" she asked.

Papa happily obliged, then told Ben and Kate to get in the picture too. Then, like a mother duck, Christina herded the group on to Willowdell Arch.

"There he is!" Grant shouted, bolting toward the statue. Christina took off after him. The others caught up quickly. Grant and Christina were petting the bronze statue of the famous husky when they arrived.

"What do you know about Balto?" Papa asked, as he studied the statue. The bronze husky's nose, face, and paws were worn and shiny from millions of children—and adults—lovingly petting the heroic dog. Christina started to tell Papa what she knew, but Grant elbowed her. "I want to tell!" he cried. Christina closed her mouth.

"Balto was a sled dog. He led his team across Alaska to save the town of Nome from a cafeteria infection," he said proudly.

"Dip-THER-i-a," Christina corrected quietly.

"Whateveria!" Grant said.

Statues!

It's Balto!

"Never mind," Christina said. She walked away from the statue a little bit and took out her New York survival guide.

"What are you looking for?" Ben asked.

"Milk," Christina replied. "Where can I get milk around here?"

"The dairy is that way," Ben said, pointing toward Willowdell Arch. "It's the Visitor's Center now, but it used to be a real dairy back in the 1800s."

"Hey, everybody!" Christina called. "Let's go to the Dairy!" She pranced off, heading into a stone tunnel. A plaque mounted on one wall read: "Willowdell Arch, constructed in 1861."

Grant, Ben and Kate caught up to her.

"Hey! What was the clue?" Kate asked.

"*Milk-ball*," Christina said. "I don't get it."

"Well," Ben said, "I think you're right on track, separating the clue into two words."

At the Dairy, they wandered around aimlessly, looking for a carton of milk, or a ball, or a package of malted milk balls, or even a ball of dried milk—anything that could constitute a clue! But there was nothing.

It's Balto!

To The Dairy!

Christina sat down on a bench with Grant and shared her box of malted milk balls. She had purchased the last box of them from a vending machine.

"I hope someone else didn't buy and eat our clue," Grant said.

"Me, too," Christina said. "If somebody did, we've come as far as we can."

"And the torch will be gone forever!" Grant cried.

Christina shook her head. The Dairy was a small place. There weren't a lot of places to hide clues. "Oh, it's hopeless!" Christina exclaimed, throwing her hands up in the air. "Utterly hopeless!"

They sat on the bench eating their malted milk balls in silence. Ben and Kate, shaking their heads to show that they too, had found nothing, came and sat down next to them. What a sight this must be, Christina thought. Four completely hopeless kids sitting on a park bench, looking like we just lost the World Series.

Christina stood up. One of her shoes felt loose, so she turned and propped her foot up on the bench.

She tied one shoe, then the other—just in case. And when she looked up, she nearly fell over backwards in surprise!

"Ooop!" she cried, clamping a hand over her mouth.

To The Dairy!

Another Clue!

For there in a glass-enclosed bulletin board lay the clue they had been searching for! The little white address label read:

RCF-DV-79S

Not particularly helpful by itself, she thought. But it was what the clue was *stuck on* that got her really excited!

With a mischievous smile, she asked the group, "Who wants to go to a baseball game?"

Another Clue!

MILK

To The Ball Game?

13 TAKE ME OUT TO THE BALL GAME!

"Ben," Papa said gratefully, "thanks for getting us these fantastic seats!"

"Yhuhhh!" Grant said, with a mouthful of popcorn, "Thhhhnks!"

"Grant. . ." Mimi said, scoldingly.

Ben's family, die-hard Yankees fans, had season tickets for seats just seven rows up from the Yankees' dugout.

"LADIES AND GENTLEMEN, CHILDREN AND BASEBALL FANS OF ALL AGES!" the Yankee Stadium announcer said over the loudspeakers. "PLEASE DIRECT YOUR ATTENTION TO THE LEFT FIELD LINE AS WE INTRODUCE TONIGHT'S VISITING TEAM, THE BOSTON RED SOX!"

Amid the cheers and boos (the boos were louder, of course), Kate said, "This is incredible! I have never been

Yankee
Stadium

Yankees vs.
Red Sox

to a baseball game before! The sights, the sounds, the smells!"

"It smells like people," Mimi commented. "Lots of people!"

"It smells like popcorn," Grant said, and hauled another handful to his mouth.

"It smells like hot dogs," Ben said, and bit into his third wiener of the day.

"It smells like beer," Papa said. Mimi frowned.

"It smells. . . like a baseball game!" Christina said.

"Well, whatever it smells like, it is wonderful!" Kate gushed joyfully. "I am sooo happy!"

Christina smiled at her like they were old friends. Christina was happy too, because she knew *exactly* where to look for the next clue, and *exactly* when it was going to appear.

On the way to the stadium, the kids had figured out that 'RCF' meant Right Center Field. 'DV' referred to the Diamond Vision screen in right centerfield. Lastly, and most importantly, '7IS' meant Seventh Inning Stretch. It was a good thing Ben was such a baseball buff!

"LADIES AND GENTLEMEN, BASEBALL FANS OF ALL AGES!" the announcer said again, "PLEASE DIRECT YOUR ATTENTION TO THE RIGHT FIELD

Yankees vs. Red Sox

Smells Like Baseball

LINE AS WE INTRODUCE YOUR HOMETOWN NEW YORK YANKEES!!"

The roar from the crowd was deafening! Not a single person remained in their seats. Even Christina jumped up and down! What was left of Grant's popcorn flew everywhere as he, too, jumped up and down to cheer for the Yankees—though he couldn't really see anything behind all the taller people standing in front of him.

"AND NOW," the announcer said in a more reverent tone, "PLEASE RISE AND REMOVE YOUR HATS, AND DIRECT YOUR ATTENTION TO HOME PLATE FOR THE SINGING OF THE NATIONAL ANTHEM."

Instantly, Yankee Stadium became as quiet as the New York Public Library's famous Reading Room. At first, the only sound was the low voice of a beautiful woman, but then the spectators—especially Papa!—joined in to sing,

> *O say, can you see,*
> *by the dawn's early light,*
> *what so proudly we hailed*
> *at the twilight's last gleaming*
> *Whose broad stripes and bright stars,*
> *through the perilous fight,*
> *o'er the ramparts we watched*

Smells Like
Baseball

National
Anthem

were so gallantly streaming.
And the rockets' red glare,
the bombs bursting in air,
gave proof through the night
that our flag was still there.
O, say does that star-spangled
banner yet wave?
O'er the land of the free,
And the home of the brave!

Christina wiped a tear from her eye as thunderous applause echoed throughout the stadium. The *Star Spangled Banner* always made her cry. Papa, too.

It was a great game so far, Christina thought as the seventh inning got underway. The Yankees were walloping their long-time rivals 12 to 2. Throughout the previous six innings, Ben had shared his seemingly-infinite knowledge of the Yankees and Yankee Stadium.

Christina, Grant, and Kate learned that the original stadium had been built in 1922–23, in a record 284 working days for only $2.5 million. . . that the massive ballpark was the first to be called a stadium, since its seating capacity

National
Anthem

Yankee
Records

was more than 70,000. . . and, among many other things, that it was called 'The House That Ruth Built' because George Herman 'Babe' Ruth—the Sultan of Swat, the Bambino—put on such a show of hitting home runs that seats at Yankee Stadium regularly sold out.

Christina waved her big souvenir foam finger in the air and yelled, "Strike 'em out! Strike 'em out! Waaay out!"

Grant, wearing a kid-size Yankees cap, waved *his* big foam finger in the air, too, but all he could do was laugh at Christina.

"Oooh! Here's the pitch!" Christina said.

The batter swung and launched the baseball to right field, where it was easily caught for out number one.

"YYYAAAYYY!!" Christina and Grant yelled.

"Here's the wind, and the pitch!" Grant called, as the next batter stood at home plate. "Strike one! Whoohoo!"

They cheered even harder when the second batter struck out swinging! The third proved to be more trouble than the first two, though, knocking more than a few foul balls into the stands.

"Come on, strike 'im out!" Christina yelled.

"Two out, nobody on, count's full! Strike him out!" Ben yelled.

"Here's the pitch!" Kate cried.

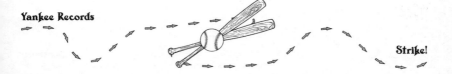

Yankee Records

Strike!

"STRUCK HIM OUT!" they all yelled, as the relieved Yankees jogged to their dugout. Christina immediately focused her attention on the Diamond Vision screen.

"LADIES AND GENTLEMEN! BASEBALL FANS OF ALL AGES, PLEASE JOIN US IN SINGING THAT OLD-TIME SEVENTH-INNING STRETCH CLASSIC, TAKE ME OUT TO THE BALL GAME!"

Christina and the others joined the thousands of raucous fans in singing, as loud as they could,

> *Take me out to the ball game,*
> *Take me out with the crowd!*
> *Buy me some peanuts and Cracker Jack,*
> *I don't care if I never get back!*
> *Let me root, root, root for the home team,*
> *If they don't win it's a shame!*
> *For it's one, two, three strikes, you're out,*
> *At the old ball game!*

And, as thunderous applause echoed once again through the stadium, the Diamond Vision screen changed to display this message:

Puzzled? Read the Daily News!

Strike!

Puzzled?

14 THE PAPER MAN COMETH

Christina lay awake in the darkness of the bedroom. She knew that she could not let harm befall the Statue of Liberty's torch. She felt as if the Statue of Liberty was imitating Smokey the Bear, saying, "Only *you* can save my torch!" instead of "Only *you* can prevent forest fires!"

Christina wondered if they should call the police and tell them what they knew. But since nobody had reported the torch missing, the police would probably dismiss her as a prankster.

She decided, based upon past experience, to let things play out. But if they couldn't solve the mystery soon, she knew she would have to tell Mimi and Papa.

She looked at the clock on the dresser—it was just after four a.m.

Way too early to get up, she thought. *Yawn.* In the

Puzzled?

Unreported Torch Theft

next bed, Grant snored. *Zznnnaack!* Are the newspapers out yet, Christina wondered. Even if they were, where would I get one?

Christina got out of bed and padded over to the window. She knew that the window faced the street—this bedroom was right over the front of the restaurant. She pushed aside the heavy draperies and was nearly blinded, for even though it was the wee hours of the morning, Little Italy was brilliantly illuminated.

Christina saw a truck rumble up the street and stop in front of a deli across the street. Painted on the side of the truck were the words DAILY NEWS.

HA! What luck! Christina thought. She watched as a man jumped out of the open back and deposited a stack of papers at the door of the deli. He hopped back in and the truck slowly rolled halfway up the block before stopping again.

Christina let the drapes fall back, and the room got *very* dark. She crawled back into bed knowing *exactly* where she would be going first thing in the morning!

Unreported
Torch Theft

The Daily
News!

15 WHERE'S THE CLUE!?!

"It's not in this paper!" Christina cried. "What are we going to do?"

It was seven a.m. The kids were sprawled on Ben's bedroom floor. They had searched the *Daily News* for the next clue, assuming that it would be a puzzle like the day before. But there was nothing.

"What if it was in yesterday's paper?" Grant suggested. "The clue at the ball game didn't say which paper to look in."

"Omigosh!" Christina cried. "What if they're all gone?"

Ben quickly jumped to his feet. "They're *not* all gone!" he said. "Wait right here!" He ran from the bedroom. It seemed like an eternity before he returned. When he did, he had a copy of the previous day's *Daily*

The Daily News!

NEWS!

Not In This Paper

News. He tossed it on the floor, and like a pack of hungry sharks, Christina, Grant, and Kate tore into it.

Sure enough, just a minute or two into the search, there they found puzzle!

> *The Game's Afoot!*
> *You know what to do.*
> *The topic is: They're Coming to America*
>
> *Streamers of hope __*
> *Faster than wind can push __*
> *Economy seats in __*
> *__ (anticipate) for freedom in the __*

"I need a pen," Christina said.

Ben snatched a pen from his desk.

"Hmmm. . . *Streamers of hope,*" she mumbled. "The topic is *They're Coming to America.* Who is?" she thought out loud.

"The immigrants!" Kate supplied. "Remember the yarn?"

Streamers of hope   y ⟨a⟩ r ⓝ

In Yesterday's
Paper

NEWS!

The Game's
Afoot!

What about this?

"What's *Faster than wind can push*?" she asked.
"Steamships!" Grant answered.

Faster than wind can push

(s)(t)e__a__[m]__s__h__i__[p]

"Where were the *economy seats*?"
"With the animals and the cargo down in steerage,"
Ben said.
"Hee hee!" Christina giggled, as she filled in the
next mystery word:

Economy seats in

◇s◇ t__ [e] [e] r__a__g__ ◇e◇

"Huh. . . *anticipate freedom in the—blank*," she said.
"What's another word for 'anticipate'?" She opened her
brain's thesaurus, but the pages were blank! Too early in
the morning, she thought.
"Four letters. . ." Ben muttered. "What are you
doing if you're anticipating something?"
"You're *waiting* for something to happen!" Christina
said. "So where did the immigrants wait?" She tried to
remember the inside of Ellis Island's immigrant depot.

The Game's
Afoot!

Immigrants?

"Aha!" she exclaimed, and completed the last mystery words:

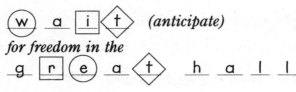

w a i t *(anticipate)*

for freedom in the

g r e a t h a l l

"YAAYY!" They all cheered.

"Ben! Get your Scrabble game!" Christina commanded.

Once again, the tiles were spilled out of their sack, clattering on the hardwood floor. In just minutes, they rearranged the letters to make:

Immigrants?

Jumble
Puzzle

"The Empire State Building!" she exclaimed. "I guess we have to get on top and look northwest!"

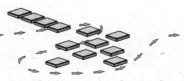

Jumble Puzzle

Empire State Building

16 STANDING AT THE TOP OF THE WORLD

Christina wiggled with anticipation as the elevator began its trip to the 86th floor of the tallest building in Manhattan. They listened to a brief history of the Empire State Building, narrated by a voice coming from speakers overhead.

"The Empire State Building is the Art Deco-flavored vision of William Lamb, hired by John Jacob Raskob, former vice president of General Motors, and former presidential candidate Alfred E. Smith. Construction began on the 1,250-foot building two weeks before Black Thursday, October 24, 1929, the day of the Great Stock Market Crash and the beginning of the Great Depression.

"60,000 tons of steel, 10 million bricks, and 200,000 cubic feet of stone became the Empire State Building in only 19 months. Sadly, 14 lives were lost during construction. For 45

Empire State
Building

Up To The
Observatory

years, until the construction of the World Trade Center's Twin Towers, this was the tallest building in the world.

"*Today, the Empire State Building boasts over 25,000 tenants and 40,000 daily visitors. Lightning strikes the 204-foot mast atop the building 500 times per year, on average.*

"*You have now reached the 86th Floor Observatory. We hope you enjoy your visit.*"

And with that, the elevator doors opened. As the elevator's passengers cleared out, Christina dragged Grant past the gift shop to the doors of the terrace.

"Hey! Slow down! You're twisting my arm! HEY!" Grant cried. Christina stopped and stared in awe at New York City, sprawled out around them in all its magnificence.

"Wow, Grant!" she exclaimed. "Look at that view!"

They walked all the way around the terrace as Ben pointed out the Flatiron Building, and way beyond that, the Statue of Liberty. He indicated the Met Life Building, and behind that, the slanted roof of the CitiCorp Building. He showed them the New York Public Library nestled among all the towering skyscrapers.

Ben stopped at the northwest corner of the terrace. Fortunately, the crowd was a little thinner here than at the three other corners.

"All right," Christina said. "We have to find that

Up To The
Observatory

Look At
That View!

clue!" They searched up and down, left and right, high and low.

"A clue!" Grant said, standing on the footrest of the closest observation binoculars.

"You see a clue? Where?" Christina said, her eyes darting around.

"Right there!" Grant said.

"Where!?" Christina shouted.

"On the fence!" Grant shouted back.

Christina looked at the fence. "Aha! There it is! On the fencepost!"

And there it was, a little white address label with a drawing of some kind, and four letters:

"Ben! Kate!" Christina shouted. "Come here! We found it!"

Ben and Kate rushed over and followed Christina's pointing finger to the clue. They looked at the odd sketch.

"It looks like a drawing of a city skyline," Kate said. "A very small section of it!"

"Yes!" Ben said. "You know what we need now?" he

Look At That View!

A Clue!

asked with a smile.

Christina and Grant, mouths agape and eyes wide, waited for the answer.

Ben put a hand in a pocket and pulled out a bunch of coins. "Some handy-dandy quarters for a close-up view!"

He fed the machine enough quarters to open the lens, and Grant, still clinging to the binoculars, peered through the eyepieces.

"Eww! Everything's blurry!" he complained. "And all I can see is sky!"

"You're too short to see the skyline, Grant," Christina told him. "I'm sorry. . . Why don't we let Ben look; he's tallest."

Dejected, Grant climbed down from the binoculars. Ben took his place. "Where should I start?" Ben asked.

"How about due northwest?" Christina suggested. "You can line up the tick marks at the base," she said, pointing to compass directions engraved on the binoculars.

"Good idea!" Ben said. He turned the binoculars until they were aimed northwest. He peeled the label off the fencepost and stuck it right between the eyepieces. He spent several minutes looking at the skyline until he had to put more quarters in.

"Hey, kid!" a gruff voice shouted. "Why don't you

A Clue!

Scanning
The Skyline

give somebody else a turn?" Christina turned to see a big, burly man who hadn't shaved recently standing behind them. He had a mean, angry look on his face as he slowly walked toward them.

Ben was frozen in place, his quarters clutched in one fist. Kate backed up to the fence, eyes wide with fear. Grant grabbed his sister's arm and hid behind her, hoping she would back away from the big, scary man.

"You've had enough time! You're not the only ones up here, you know! So scram!" he growled.

"HEY! Leave those kids alone!" growled a voice that sounded just as gruff. Papa came out of nowhere and stood between the four trembling kids and the mean old ogre. "There's another set of binoculars over there! Go use 'em!" Papa ordered.

The man growled and stalked away, grumbling about no-good kids with no respect.

Papa turned to the kids, and said, "Boy, some people. . ."

"Yeah. Some people. . ." Grant echoed, showing a little bravery from behind Christina-the-shield.

Ben shakily finished feeding the binoculars, and went back to scanning the skyline. A minute later, he cried, "Got it!"

Scanning The Skyline

Some People. . .

"Where?!" Christina asked. "I want to see!" Ben stood aside and helped Christina up on the footrest so she could see. Being careful to not move the binoculars, she looked at the clue and then the center of the field-of-vision.

"Is that an airplane?" she asked, confused.

"It is," Ben said. "On the deck of the *USS Intrepid*!"

Some
People...

To The
Intrepid!

17 FLIGHTS OF FANCY

When they reached the *USS Intrepid* (after begging Mimi and Papa to take them there) Christina was finally able to ask the rest of the group what they thought 'GHWB' might be. But nobody had an answer.

"Gosh, I hope we don't have to search the whole ship!" Christina cried. "That would take days!"

"Hey kids!" Papa called out. "We've got the tickets! Let's go see the ship!" As they waited to pass through security, Christina darted out of line to grab a guide to the ship's exhibits.

Papa, an ex-Army guy and military history buff, told them the history of the *Intrepid*.

"The *Intrepid* is a World War II-era aircraft carrier," he explained. "She took part in some of the most important battles of World War II in the Pacific Ocean.

To The Intrepid

Search The Ship?

She was bombed seven times, attacked by kamikaze pilots five times, and hit by one torpedo. But she kept coming back! The Japanese called her *The Ghost Ship*."

"Cool! A ghost ship!" Grant said.

"In the 1960s," Papa continued, "she was the prime recovery vessel for NASA's Mercury and Gemini capsules. Later, she served in the Vietnam War. She wrapped up her active service as an anti-submarine warfare ship and was retired in 1974."

"When did she become a museum?" Christina asked.

"In 1982, the *Intrepid* Sea-Air-Space museum opened," Papa said. "The *Intrepid* Museum Foundation saved the ship from being scrapped. There are hundreds of exhibits on board!"

"But I can't find the one I'm looking for," Christina muttered.

"Which one is that?" Papa asked.

Phooey, Christina thought, I was hoping he didn't hear me, but maybe he'll know!

"Umm. . . all I've got is initials: 'G-H-W-B'," Christina said sheepishly.

Papa laughed. "That's easy! George Herbert Walker Bush! He flew a Grumman TBM-3E Avenger

Search The
Ship?

George H. W.
Bush!?!

torpedo bomber in World War II!"

Christina was elated! "That's it! Thank you, Papa!" She turned to Grant, Ben, and Kate and winked. "Papa knew!"

It took a while to make it to the *Intrepid's* hangar deck, where the Avenger torpedo-bomber was on exhibit. The crowds moved through the museum about as quickly as molasses in Alaska in January.

The Avenger was perched upon its own landing gear, its wings folded back, just as it would have been stored during active duty. Its bomb bay doors were folded open and a mirror was placed underneath, angled just right so that you could see the interior of the bomb bay as you stood in front of the information plaque.

Christina and the clue-hunters scanned every square inch of the aircraft that they could see—but the clue was not visible!

"I hope it's not in the cockpit," Grant said.

"It can't be," Christina said. "All the other clues have been pretty much in plain sight. It's here—it's got to be."

"Christina. . ." Kate said expectantly. "I think I see it!"

George H. W. Bush!?!

To The Avenger!

"Where?"

"In the mirror," Kate replied.

Christina looked closely at the mirror. She saw the little white address label stuck *way* up inside the bomb bay!

"It's too far away to read! And it's backwards!" Christina cried. "How are we going to get the clue?" She looked around the hangar deck. There were too many people—including Mimi and Papa—too close by for one of them to get underneath the aircraft. To make matters worse, there was a security guard standing nearby. She would be on the scene before any of them could even hope to get under the plane. Think, think, think!

The gears of her mind turning, Christina thought and thought as the other three kids squinted at the mirror, trying to read the clue. Then, all at once, the perfect plan unfolded in her imagination!

Christina kneeled, took Grant by the arm, and whispered in his ear. Grant listened intently. A smile spread across his face, and then he laughed quietly.

"Okay, kids, let's get a move on!" Mimi said. "There's lots more to see!"

"Okay! Just a minute, please," Christina said. "I'm writing in my field journal."

"All right," Mimi said. "We're going to walk over to

To The Avenger!

In The Bomb Bay!?!

this next group of exhibits. Don't take too long!"

The second Mimi turned around, Christina whispered to Grant, "GO!"

Grant spun on his heel and walked directly to the exhibit across the aisle. He pretended to look at the informational plaque for that exhibit for a few seconds, then turned back to face the Avenger.

"Hey! Christina! I gotta show you something!" Grant shouted, as he dashed toward the plane.

Grant pretended to trip over the chain surrounding the plane, causing a loud racket. The mirror skittered out from under the plane, and Grant slid to a stop, landing on his back directly underneath the bomb bay.

He lay there for a few seconds. To the security guard, it looked like an accident. But Grant was reading the clue!

The security guard helped Grant out from under the plane, and asked if he was hurt. Grant moaned and groaned, but nodded that he was okay. He winked at Christina as Mimi and Papa returned to hurry him out of harm's way.

In The Bomb
Bay!?!

Crafty Little
Devils!

18 No Time Like the Present

"What?!" Christina cried. "We could NEVER get there in time! We probably couldn't even get off this stupid boat by then! We're doomed!"

Grant had waited until Mimi and Papa got a little ahead of the kids before he told them the clue:

Make time for the big square screen
1500h

Ben had quickly deduced that the clue referred to the big TV screen in Times Square, and that '1500h' meant 15:00 hours, or 3 p.m. Something was going to appear on the Jumbotron in Times Square soon—and they needed to be there!

"Oh, GOSH! What are we going to do?!" Christina

Times Square?

What Do We Do?

115

wailed.

Ben's cell phone rang. He looked at the display to see who was calling.

"Vinny! It's Vinny!" Ben shouted. "HE can get there in time if he leaves right NOW!"

"Vinny!" Ben answered the phone. He listened for a second, then gave Vinny *very* specific instructions. Ben ended the call and said, "Vinny's going to get there in time. I think we can relax a little now."

"Maybe you can, but I can't!" Christina said in desperation. "That torch is going to be lost if we don't get that clue!" She was practically in tears.

Ben put a comforting hand on her shoulder. "Christina. . . we can count on Vinny, I promise you. He's *never* let me down, not even once."

Christina looked at Ben with her bottom lip stuck out.

"I hope so, Ben, I hope so."

What Do We Do?

Send Vinny!

19 A FOURTH TO REMEMBER

"*We interrupt this broadcast with breaking news,*" the news anchor said. "*An original torch from the Statue of Liberty is missing. It was taken by cargo ship from Liberty Island three days ago to be refurbished.*

"*The crate was unloaded at a pier in Queens. The crate, which should have contained the 1916 torch, was filled instead. . . with. . . frozen fish. Workers opened the crate this morning when they noticed water leaking and a . . . fishy smell coming from the crate.*

"*Police, the FBI, and other state and federal agencies are on the case, examining the crate and a potential crime scene at Liberty Island. A spokesman for the NYPD stated that a note to contact the kidnappers, along with a clue, was left in the crate, but did not release any further details. We will bring you more of this incredible story as it unfolds. We now*

Breaking News!

Torch Taken!

117

return you to the regularly scheduled programming."

Papa, Mimi, and the other adults in the family restaurant were shocked into silence by the terrible news. They were so stunned that they didn't notice Christina, Grant, Ben and Kate walk right out the front door.

"Well, there you have it," Christina said. "The news is out. People all over the country—all over the world!—know that the torch is missing!"

"And all *we* can do is *wait*," Grant added. "Bummer!"

Vinny had arrived at Times Square at 2:57, according to the time below the Jumbotron screen, and he had intently watched for anything out of the ordinary. Nothing strange appeared at 3 pm, but at 3:30 pm, this message appeared:

Be back in 24 hours. Give or take . . .

Torch Taken!

24 Hours?

20 Sittin' on the Dock of the Bay

Twenty-four hours after the message appeared on the Jumbotron in Times Square, Christina, Grant, Ben, and Kate were nowhere near Times Square.

Instead, the kids were gathered around the computer in Ben's bedroom, watching a live webcam broadcast from a building opposite the Jumbotron in Times Square. At 3:00, this message appeared:

Have you been following our leads?
You know what you're looking for
We hope you're not scared of numbers
For this one's pilings are keepers of the flame

"Good grief!" Christina exclaimed. "Are these people talking to *us*?"

24 Hours?

Message for Us?

119

"Sure seems like it!" Ben said. "So, where's this clue going to take us?"

"Well," Christina said, "what numbers are people afraid of? Specifically, what *one* number?"

Grant, Ben, and Kate looked at each other, then they shouted, "THIRTEEN!"

"Yup!" Christine said, smiling from ear to ear—for she already knew where to go!

"And piers have pilings!" Ben said.

"PIER 13!" they all shouted.

In a lucky twist of fate, the riverboat they were taking out into the East River for the fireworks show was docked at Pier 13. Vinny dropped them off as close as he could.

The number of pedestrians along the waterfront was amazing! People were crammed into the streets tighter than Styrofoam peanuts stuffed in a bag being stepped on by an elephant! Thankfully, unless you had a reason to be on a particular pier, you weren't getting on it. Papa handed each of the kids a special Pier 13 Riverboat Pass encased in plastic and attached to a ball chain. They put them over their necks and stepped through the gates onto the far-less-crowded Pier 13.

Message For Us?

To Pier 13!

The Riverboat was halfway down the pier. Christina and Grant took the left side, Ben and Kate the right side, and together they scanned every vessel very carefully for anything that could contain Lady Liberty's old torch. By the time they reached the gangway to the Pier 13 Riverboat, they had seen nothing. The twilight's quick fade to darkness did not help.

They regrouped across the pier from the riverboat and pretended to study a private yacht docked there.

"We have to keep going down the pier," Christina said urgently.

"How do we know we haven't walked right by it?" Kate said.

"Yeah," Ben said, "there are a lot of big boats out here that could easily hold ten torches."

Christina grunted in frustration. "But remember what the riddle at the beginning of this mystery said? *By the rockets' glare.* I take that to mean that if we don't find the torch by the time the fireworks start, it's going to be in Davy Jones' Locker before the second round of rockets goes up.

"And," she explained, "if they're going to dump it,

To Pier 13!

Have To Keep Going

then it has to be ready to dump. It can't be down in a cargo hold when the fireworks start in. . ." —she looked at her Carole Marsh Mysteries watch— "less than 30 minutes!"

"Christina, Grant, Ben, Kate!" Papa yelled. "Let's go, the boat's leaving in 15 minutes!"

"We can't go yet!" Christina said under her breath.

She ran to Papa and put on her prettiest give-me-whatever-I-want smile. "Papa! Can we go take a quick look down the end of the pier? Please?! We won't take long and you can see us from the deck of the riverboat! I *promise* we'll just go and come right back. We just want a quick look!"

Papa always gave in to that face. He sighed and said it would be okay—but to hurry, because they did *not* want to be left behind!

"Thanks, Papa!" Christina yelled, and the kids took off running, searching the pier frantically as darkness fell.

"Christina! I think I see it!" Ben called. Ben and Kate stood atop a tall stairway that went up and over the side of a small cargo ship very similar—just painted red instead of white—to the one that had taken the torch off Liberty Island.

As Christina and Grant reached the bottom of the stairs, Ben shouted to them, "I think this is it! The torch has to be under this—WHOA!"

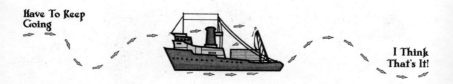

Have To Keep Going

I Think That's It!

I think I can see it. . .

"AAAAHHHH!!" Kate screamed.

Christina and Grant halted their charge up the stairs as Ben and Kate disappeared from sight, yanked down onto the ship by unseen hands!

"Omigosh!" Christina cried. Ben and Kate's sudden disappearance almost guaranteed that this was where the torch was. She had to save them! And the torch! "Grant, stay here! It's not safe for you!" Christina warned. Grant looked at her like she was nuts.

"It's not safe for you, either!" Grant cried, as his brave big sister slinked up the steps as quickly as she could.

Perched ten feet above the pier, Christina peeked over the edge of the ship's hull. She saw a crate certainly big enough to contain the torch, and saw Ben and Kate being held down on the deck by two big men as another tried to tie them up! Their cries for help were drowned out by the noise of some machinery's motor running somewhere nearby.

Christina quickly looked around the deck and saw no one else. The men manhandling Ben and Kate were completely distracted. Christina climbed up the rest of the steps, swung her legs over the handrails, and with a quick glance back at Grant, slid down the other side.

She landed on the deck and scurried into the

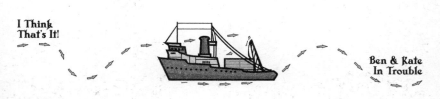

I Think
That's It!

Ben & Kate
In Trouble

shadows as Ben nearly broke free. One of the men caught him near the torch, and tossed him back to the others.

Christina looked up above the deck and saw, suspended from the crane's arm, a huge net full of something that was dripping all over the deck. And it was right over where the men were holding Ben and Kate!

She followed the crane's arm down to the control room toward the stern of the ship. The men were still distracted as they restrained Ben and Kate. Christina made a mad dash from the shadows for the control room, and slipped inside.

Christina scanned the glowing buttons and dials of the control panel. She looked frantically for the button that would release the cargo suspended from the crane.

"Hey! There's another one at the crane controls!" one of the men shouted.

Christina, scared out of her wits, hands shaking, found what she was looking for: a big red button marked EMERGENCY RELEASE, underneath a little latched cover.

She tried to pry the cover off, but it was stuck! She looked back up, and the man with the rope was turning around!

"Hey! What are you doing?" a voice cried, and that was all the distraction Christina needed.

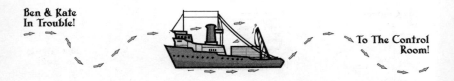

Ben & Kate
In Trouble!

To The Control
Room!

All three men turned toward the stairs, where Grant now stood at the top.

The latch on the button released!

Christina flipped it open, yelled "LOOK UP!!" as loud as she could, and mashed the button into the control panel.

Time seemed to stop for just two seconds as a loud warning buzzer sounded. The men looked up, startled by the sound of impending danger, and instinctively released Ben and Kate. The net dropped very slowly at first, and then time returned to normal. . .

KERSPLAT!!

Ben dragged Kate out of the way just as hundreds of pounds of thawing fish crashed down upon the three bad guys. Still-frozen fish skittered across the deck, leaving trails of fishy ice water and other goo!

Christina dashed out of the control room and headed for the stairs. Ben and Kate were already over the top. She clambered up the stairs and slid down the other side just as Papa reached the bottom of the stairs.

"WHAT were you doing on that boat?!" he roared. "I let you go off down the pier and you start climbing around on ships where you have no business!!"

To The Control Room!

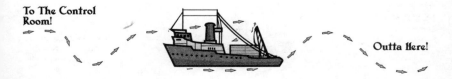

Outta Here!

"PAPA!" Christina yelled back. "The Statue of Liberty's torch is on that ship!"

"Yeah, right!" Papa said. He was too angry to really hear what she had just said. He picked up Grant and stormed off, headed back for the riverboat.

Christina, Ben, and Kate followed him, not believing what had just happened.

"But Papa doesn't believe me," Christina cried.

Papa put Grant down and ushered him up the ramp. He glared at Ben and Kate as they slipped by. Papa grabbed Christina by the arm and hauled her up the ramp. The man checking passes pulled the ramp away from the boat and released the stern line.

As the Pier 13 Riverboat moved slowly away from the pier, Christina saw one last chance to save the torch— one of "New York's finest" came up to talk to the dockman.

"Officer!" Christina shouted. "Liberty's torch is on that red ship! There are men on board guarding it!"

The NYPD officer looked up at the riverboat.

"SAVE THE TORCH ON THE RED SHIP!" she yelled as loudly as she could.

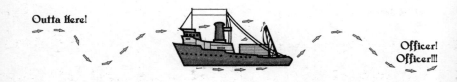

Outta Here!

Officer!
Officer!!!

21 SAILING AWAY

Quite like the rest of their trip, the day was clear and sunny. A light breeze tickled the leaves of the trees. Mimi sat with Christina on a park bench overlooking the Model Boat Pond in Central Park as Christina clipped the front page story out of the *Daily News,* the *New York Post,* and the *New York Times*. Grant, Ben, Kate, and Papa were at the water's edge, watching the model boats racing on the pond.

With the news coverage that the recovery of the Statue of Liberty's torch was getting, you might have thought that nothing else in the world was newsworthy. Christina tucked the thick wad of newspaper clippings into her red three-ring binder-slash-notebook.

"You could have just put the whole newspaper in there!" Mimi said.

Clipping The
News

Torch
Recovery

Christina laughed. She could have!

"So, Christina, give me gist of the story," Mimi requested.

"Well, it boils down to this," Christina began. "A bunch of people from other countries wanted to protest the strict immigration rules the United States set in place after September 11, 2001. They used all the legal means possible to get their families into the United States, but they failed.

"So they cooked up this scheme to take a symbol of America's freedom and hold it hostage. The torch's refurbishment project was the perfect cover."

"That *was* a good cover operation," Mimi commented.

Christina continued, "The news should have been out on Tuesday, when the torch was taken off Liberty Island. However, the cargo ship arrived at the dock too late—after taking too much time switching the crates—and the crew at the refurbishment company had gone home. No one did anything with the crate until it started leaking, two days later."

"Did the papers say what the kidnappers left in the crate for clues?" Mimi asked.

"Yes, ma'am!" Christina said. "They left a note to contact the group's leader to discuss terms for returning

Torch Recovery

Cover Operation

the statue's torch. The note just said, 'Puzzled? Read the *Daily News!*' And there were a series of clues that led us— I mean, would have led investigators—on a wild tour of the city!"

"Hmmm," Mimi said. "I didn't read about a series of clues in the paper, Christina." She gave her granddaughter a suspicious smile. "Is there something you want to tell me?"

Christina sighed. "Well," she confessed, "there was a puzzle in that day's paper . . ."

"And . . ." Mimi prompted.

Christina opened her notebook to show her the first puzzle that would soon end up in Mimi's latest mystery for kids—*The Mystery in New York City!*

The End

Cover
Operation

NEWS!

Puzzled?

ABOUT THE AUTHOR

Carole Marsh is an author and publisher who has written many works of fiction and non-fiction for young readers. She travels throughout the United States and around the world to research her books. In 1979 Carole Marsh was named Communicator of the Year for her corporate communications work with major national and international corporations.

Marsh is the founder and CEO of Gallopade International, established in 1979. Today, Gallopade International is widely recognized as a leading source of educational materials for every state and many countries. Marsh and Gallopade were recipients of the 2004 Teachers' Choice Award. Marsh has written more than 50 Carole Marsh Mysteries™. In 2007, she was named Georgia Author of the Year. Years ago, her children, Michele and Michael, were the original characters in her mystery books. Today, they continue the Carole Marsh Books tradition by working at Gallopade. By adding grandchildren Grant and Christina as new mystery characters, she has continued the tradition for a third generation.

Ms. Marsh welcomes correspondence from her readers. You can e-mail her at fanclub@gallopade.com, visit carolemarshmysteries.com, or write to her in care of Gallopade International, P.O. Box 2779, Peachtree City, Georgia, 30269 USA.

Built-In Book Club
Talk About It!

1. Who was your favorite character in the mystery? Why?

2. If you were able to visit New York City, what places would you like to visit?

3. How do you think early immigrants to the United States must have felt when their ship sailed into New York Harbor and they finally saw the Statue of Liberty?

4. Why do you think New York is called "the city that never sleeps?"

5. What was your favorite part of the book? Why?

6. Why did using the Scrabble game letters help the kids unscramble the words more easily?

7. Why did hearing the Star Spangled Banner make Christina and Papa cry? Do you know anyone else who is affected by that song in the same way?

8. What do you like most about reading mysteries?

Built-In Book Club
Bring It To Life!

1. Map it Out! Find a map of the United States. List the
   states that Grant and Christina would have traveled
   through if they had driven from your state to New York
   City. After you list the states, make a new list and put
   them in alphabetical order. Then, make another list by
   size—list the smallest state first and the largest state last!

2. Put on a play! You will need four actors. Three actors
   will portray immigrants coming into the United States
   through Ellis Island. The other actor will portray an
   immigration agent asking the immigrants questions. The
   agent should ask them their names, where they came
   from, where they are going, and why they have come to
   the United States. He will decide whether each
   immigrant is admitted to the U.S. Make up interesting
   answers to the questions, use accents, wear costumes—
   make it fun!

3. Are you a city person or a small-town person? Divide your
   group into two teams—those who would like to live in a
   small town, and those who would like to live in a city like
   New York. Leave two members out of the groups to serve
   as judges. Each group should list all the advantages of
   their way of life—and be persuasive! The judges will
   decide where they would like to live based on what they
   hear from each group!

4. Create a slogan! "I Love New York" is a recent New York
   slogan. Make up a new one now that you know so much
   about New York!

Glossary

agnello: *(ahn-nello)* "lamb" in Italian, specifically, meat from a lamb

balsamico: *(bahl-sah-mee-co)* "balsamic" in Italian (in Italian, adjectives come after their nouns!)

bocconotti: *(boh-coh-noh-tee)* little pastries filled with ricotta cheese

buongiorno: *(bwon-zhor-no)* "good morning" in Italian

 cacophony: a lot of different sounds being made all at once, so that what you hear is really annoying

 corrosion: gradual decay

 pedestal: a base or support for a column, statue or vase

 philanthropist: someone who donates vast sums of money to charitable causes

 quarantine: isolation of a person or place infected with a contagious disease

SCAVENGER HUNT!

Recipe for fun: Read the book, take a tour, find the items on this list and check them off! (Hint: Look high and low!!) *Teachers: you have permission to reproduce this form for your students.*

__1. Balto

__2. an Avenger

__3. South Street Market

__4. dedication plaques

__5. Great Hall

__6. St. Patrick's Cathedral

__7. observation binoculars

__8. Guggenheim Museum

__9. *Washington Crossing the Delaware*

__10. Jumbotron

New York City

Places To Go & Things To Know!

The Statue of Liberty, Liberty Island – a symbol of American liberty and freedom, paid for and given by the French people

Ellis Island Immigration Museum – features Great Hall where immigrants were registered; names of 250,000 immigrants are engraved in the Wall of Honor which stands outside

The Metropolitan Museum of Art, Upper East Side – perhaps the most comprehensive art collection in the Western world

Saint Patrick's Cathedral, Upper Midtown – largest Catholic cathedral in the United States; construction took 38 years

Central Park – this 843-acre park was created with ten million cartloads of dirt and rock over swamps, farms, and quarries

Yankee Stadium, Bronx, – home of the Yankee baseball team; built in 1923, this New York landmark offers daily tours

The Empire State Building – New York's tallest building

Staten Island Ferry – one of the best deals for one of the best views; take the ferry at dusk to see the city skyline gradually recede into the night

The USS Intrepid Sea-Air-Space Museum, Pier 86 – features plane exhibits dating back to the 1940s, including the *U.S.S. Edson* destroyer and the USS *Growler* missile submarine

Solomon R. Guggenheim Museum, Upper East Side – world-class art museum designed by famous architect Frank Lloyd Wright

United Nations, Lower Midtown – headquarters houses Security Council, General Assembly, and Conference Building; peace bell, rose garden, statues, and Colors of the World (flags)

Rockefeller Center, Theater District – an official New York landmark, this site was nearly an opera house before John D. Rockefeller built the largest privately owned complex of its kind; site includes Radio City Music Hall and the NBC studios where the *Today Show* is filmed

Grand Central Terminal, Lower Midtown – commissioned by tycoon Cornelius Vanderbuilt, this railway station features a vaulted ceiling with constellations and elaborate sculptures; nearly half a million people pass through to the subway daily

NYCTourist.com – features a photo tour of popular New York City sites, located at: www.nyctourist.com/photo_menu.htm

Dorling Kindersley Travel Guide, New York, 2003 – Christina's New York "Survival Guide"

WRITE YOUR OWN MYSTERY!

Make up a dramatic title!

You can pick four real kid characters!

Select a real place for the story's setting!

Try writing your first draft!

Edit your first draft!

Read your final draft aloud!

You can add art, photos or illustrations!

Share your book with others and send me a copy!

Six Secret Writing tips from Carole Marsh!

CAROLE MARSH MYSTERIES™

Enjoy this exciting excerpt from

The Mystery at Disney World

1 We're Going to Disney World

"I'm going to Disneyland!" shouted Grant, jumping up and down on Christina's bed. This wasn't her brother's first trip to Disney, but he sure acted like it, his sister Christina thought.

"Grant!" she cried. "It's 5 a.m.! Go back to sleep. The park doesn't open for another four hours!" When Grant didn't stop bouncing up and down, Christina threw her pillow at Grant and knocked him down. "Go back to bed!"

Grant hopped off of Christina's bed, stuck his tongue out at his sister, and headed straight for Mimi and Papa's room in their condominium. He didn't care if the park didn't open for another *24 hours*, he wanted to be first in line. Much to Grant's surprise, Papa was sitting at the table in the kitchen reading the morning paper.

"Good morning, kiddo!" Papa said, as he sipped his cup of coffee.

"I'm going to Disneyland!" shouted Grant again.

Papa laughed and said, "Actually, you are going to Disney World. Disneyland is in Anaheim, California, and we are in Orlando, Florida."

"Oh," Grant said. "I'm going to Disney World!"

Papa just smiled and went back to reading his *Orlando Sentinel*. Christina came out of the bedroom stretching and yawning. She was just as excited about being in Orlando as Grant was. When Mimi and Papa invited Grant and Christina to go to Disney World, Christina could hardly wait. She knew that Mimi had never been to Disney World. And since Christina had been many times before—Papa called her a seasoned pro—she planned to show Mimi the ropes!

"Morning, Papa," she said, as she headed into the kitchen. Grabbing her favorite cereal, a carton of milk, and two bowls and spoons, Christina joined Grant and Papa at the table. She knew that between writing a mystery and visiting Disney World, Mimi was going to have a busy day, so she fixed breakfast for herself and Grant while Mimi slept in.

"Morning, princess," Papa said, as he finished his paper. Papa woke up early every morning—even when they were on vacation—to walk a few miles, and read the morning paper. "How did you sleep?"

"I couldn't go to sleep!" interrupted Grant. "I didn't sleep a wink!"

"Oh, and I suppose that's why you woke me up five times with your snoring last night," Christina teased.

"Did not!" Grant protested.

"Did too!" Christina shrieked.

"Did not!" Grant shouted again.

"All right, all right you two!" Papa said, as he finished his cup of coffee. "Grant, why don't you go get the map of the park, so we can plot our adventure for today!"

Papa always knew how to stop Christina and Grant from arguing.

Grant quickly ran into their bedroom to get the Magic Kingdom map that the people at Disney had sent to Mimi for her book research. Christina cleared their cereal bowls and Papa's coffee cup, and put them into the dishwasher.

When she returned to the table, Papa had already spread out the colorful map for them all to see.

"So, Christina, where do you want to go first?" Papa asked.

With no hesitation at all, Christina answered, "Tomorrowland! Space Mountain is my favorite roller coaster ever!"

"Well, I want to go to Frontierland!" insisted Grant. "Big Mountain Railroad Thunder is *my* favorite roller coaster ever!"

"Grant! It's the Big Thunder Mountain Railroad, silly." Christina laughed.

"That's what I said, Christina. The Big Mountain Railroad Thunder."

This time, Christina didn't even attempt to correct him.

"And look," Grant boasted. "I even brought my coonskin cap that I got in San Antonio at the Alamo."

Grant grinned as he put the hat on backwards so that the tail went right down the middle of his face.

"Oh, Grant! You are so silly!" Christina giggled.

"Well kids, we have all day, so don't worry, we'll make it to both attractions," Mimi said, as she joined them at the table.

"I'm sorry Mimi! Did we wake you up?" Christina said. "I told Grant not to be so loud."

"Oh, it's alright. We have a lot of planning to do and I want to be a part of it!"

Mimi always woke up in a great mood, Christina thought. Unlike Mimi, Christina didn't like getting up in the morning, especially when Grant would jump on her bed and scream at the top of his lungs. Being a human alarm clock was his favorite way to wake his sleeping sister.

"Alright, so let's make a plan!" Mimi said, her pad and pencil in hand. Christina didn't remember ever seeing her grandmother without something to write on. Usually, it was her laptop computer. But, she decided lugging a laptop around the nearly 30,000 acres of Disney World didn't sound like too much fun, so she opted for the old-fashioned way—pencil and paper.

"There are six *lands* in Disney World: Adventureland, Frontierland, Fantasyland, Tomorrowland, Mickey's Toontown Fair, and Liberty Square," said Mimi.

"Mickey's Toontown Fair and Liberty Square aren't *lands*, Mimi!" Grant laughed. He loved when he knew something the adults didn't.

"Well, although they don't have *land* in their names, that's what Walt Disney called them," Mimi corrected.

"But first you have to go through Main Street,

U.S.A," stated Christina very matter-of-factly.

"Very good, Christina," Papa said. Although he liked to help plan their trips, Christina knew that whatever Mimi wanted to do was what Papa wanted to do. "So where to first?"

"I know, I know!" Grant said, squirming in his seat. "Frontierland!"

"Well, I have an idea," said Mimi. "Why don't we go clockwise? We'll start here at Adventureland," she said as she pointed to the map, "and we'll work our way all the way around to Tomorrowland."

Christina knew that Mimi was being diplomatic. If she went counterclockwise, they would start with Christina's favorite–Tomorrowland, and Grant wouldn't be very happy about that. With Mimi's plan, they wouldn't start with anyone's favorite. And secretly she hoped that Grant would be so tired by the time they made it to Tomorrowland that he wouldn't want to ride Space Mountain with her.

"Sounds great to me!" said Grant.

"Sounds wonderful to me!" Papa agreed.

"Sounds perfect to me!" Christina said, with a laugh.

"Then we are agreed!" Mimi smiled.

All of a sudden Mimi jumped up from the table with a panicked look on her face and said, "Oh my goodness!"

"What's the matter, Mimi?" Christina said worriedly. "Did you forget something?"

"Oh, no!" Mimi gasped.

"What, *what*?" Grant insisted.

"Just look at the clock!" Mimi cried.

WOULD YOU LIKE TO BE A CHARACTER IN A CAROLE MARSH MYSTERY?

If you would like to star in a Carole Marsh Mystery, fill out the form below and write a 25-word paragraph about why you think you would make a good character! Once you're done, ask your mom or dad to send this page to:

Carole Marsh Mysteries Fan Club
Gallopade International
P.O. Box 2779
Peachtree City, GA 30269

My name is: _____

I am a: ____boy _____ girl   Age: _____

I live at: _____

City: _____ State:____ Zip code: _____

My e-mail address: _____

My phone number is: _____

_____
_____
_____
_____
_____
_____
_____
_____
_____
_____

www.carolemarshmysteries.com

- *Check out what's coming up next! Are we coming to your area with our next book release? Maybe you can have your book signed by the author!*

- *Join the Carole Marsh Mysteries Fan Club!*

- *Apply for the chance to be a character in an upcoming Carole Marsh Mystery!*

- *Learn how to write your own mystery!*